Short Sta
A Rainey Daye Cozy Mystery, book 2

by

Kathleen Suzette

Books by Kathleen Suzette:

A Rainey Daye Cozy Mystery Series

Clam Chowder and a Murder
A Rainey Daye Cozy Mystery, book 1
A Short Stack and a Murder
A Rainey Daye Cozy Mystery, book 2
Cherry Pie and a Murder
A Rainey Daye Cozy Mystery, book 3
Barbecue and a Murder
A Rainey Daye Cozy Mystery, book 4
Birthday Cake and a Murder
A Rainey Daye Cozy Mystery, book 5
Hot Cider and a Murder
A Rainey Daye Cozy Mystery, book 6
Roast Turkey and a Murder
A Rainey Daye Cozy Mystery, book 7
Gingerbread and a Murder
A Rainey Daye Cozy Mystery, book 8
Fish Fry and a Murder
A Rainey Daye Cozy Mystery, book 9
Cupcakes and a Murder
A Rainey Daye Cozy Mystery, book 10
Lemon Pie and a Murder
A Rainey Daye Cozy Mystery, book 11
Pasta and a Murder
A Rainey Daye Cozy Mystery, book 12
Chocolate Cake and a Murder
A Rainey Daye Cozy Mystery, book 13

A Pumpkin Hollow Mystery Series

Candy Coated Murder
A Pumpkin Hollow Mystery, book 1
Murderously Sweet
A Pumpkin Hollow Mystery, book 2
Chocolate Covered Murder
A Pumpkin Hollow Mystery, book 3
Death and Sweets
A Pumpkin Hollow Mystery, book 4
Sugared Demise
A Pumpkin Hollow Mystery, book 5
Confectionately Dead
A Pumpkin Hollow Mystery, book 6
Hard Candy and a Killer
A Pumpkin Hollow Mystery, book 7
Candy Kisses and a Killer
A Pumpkin Hollow Mystery, book 8
Terminal Taffy
A Pumpkin Hollow Mystery, book 9
Fudgy Fatality
A Pumpkin Hollow Mystery, book 10
Truffled Murder
A Pumpkin Hollow Mystery, book 11
Caramel Murder
A Pumpkin Hollow Mystery, book 12
Peppermint Fudge Killer
A Pumpkin Hollow Mystery, book 13
Chocolate Heart Killer
A Pumpkin Hollow Mystery, book 14

Strawberry Creams and Death
A Pumpkin Hollow Mystery, book 15
Pumpkin Spice Lies
A Pumpkin Hollow Mystery, book 16

A Freshly Baked Cozy Mystery Series

Apple Pie A La Murder,
A Freshly Baked Cozy Mystery, Book 1
Trick or Treat and Murder,
A Freshly Baked Cozy Mystery, Book 2
Thankfully Dead
A Freshly Baked Cozy Mystery, Book 3
Candy Cane Killer
A Freshly Baked Cozy Mystery, Book 4
Ice Cold Murder
A Freshly Baked Cozy Mystery, Book 5
Love is Murder
A Freshly Baked Cozy Mystery, Book 6
Strawberry Surprise Killer
A Freshly Baked Cozy Mystery, Book 7
Plum Dead
A Freshly Baked Cozy Mystery, book 8
Red, White, and Blue Murder
A Freshly Baked Cozy Mystery, book 9

A Gracie Williams Mystery Series

Pushing Up Daisies in Arizona,
A Gracie Williams Mystery, Book 1

Kicked the Bucket in Arizona,
A Gracie Williams Mystery, Book 2

A Home Economics Mystery Series

Appliqued to Death
A Home Economics Mystery, book 1

Table of Contents

Chapter One

"WELL, LOOK WHO DECIDED to show up. I thought you were dead," Georgia Johnson said with a roll of her eyes. She was standing out front of the diner, sneaking in one last smoke break before starting her shift at Sam's Diner. "Pity you aren't."

I narrowed my eyes at her. You would be right if you thought Georgia, and I weren't the best of friends.

"Thanks, Georgia. You're a regular ray of sunshine, aren't you?"

She didn't answer me as I pushed open the door to the diner and glanced at the clock behind the front counter. It was two minutes to six. Heaving a sigh of relief, I headed toward the back room. I was late, but at least I was there before we were officially open.

In my defense, it was my bed's fault. It was warm and cozy, and far too comfortable. It was late May in Sparrow, Idaho, and we had had a cold spell that had suddenly hit. It would most likely be the last cold spell before the heat of summer set in, and staying under the blankets was a temptation I couldn't resist. Plus, my boss, Sam Stevens, was too laid back. If I had to face a screaming boss, I'd be at work on time.

"Hey Rainey," Sam said from behind the grill. I could smell bacon and sausage cooking, and my stomach growled. I hadn't had time to eat before I left for work.

"Good morning, Sam," I said and went to the back room and put my purse up in a locker. I grabbed an apron and tied it around my waist and headed back to the kitchen. The bell above the door jingled as some of our regular early birds arrived.

"Gonna be a chilly one," Sam remarked as I returned to the kitchen.

"Feels that way, but I think it's the last of the cold weather," I said.

Sam really was a laid back boss, and I appreciated him more than my tardiness showed. I'd have to make it up to him somehow. I was writing another cookbook, and Sam was kind enough to agree to allow me to try out some recipes on the customers at the diner. We had struck a deal where he supplied the ingredients, and I experimented with new recipes for him to add, at least temporarily, to the menu. My blueberry tart had been a big hit, and I was trying to figure out what I would make next.

I headed out to the front counter. Old Grant Barrow sat at the front counter, his white head bent over the morning newspaper.

"Can I get you some coffee, Grant?"

"Sure," he mumbled and turned the page. "It's nippy out there. My lumbago can't handle much more of this. Seems summer comes later and later every year."

"Well, hopefully, it will be warming up soon," I said and went to make the coffee.

We had three morning regulars: Grant, Skip Darlington, and Carlisle Garlock. Skip and Carlisle were in their late fifties, and they always stopped in for coffee and breakfast before heading to their jobs. Grant had long since been retired, and he liked to spend at least the first two hours of his day nursing his coffee but rarely ordering food. I figured he was lonely and needed the company.

When the coffee was finished brewing, I filled a carafe and brought it to the front counter. Skip had taken up his usual seat near Grant and grunted a greeting. The corner counter seat was empty. I frowned.

"Carlisle must be running late this morning," I said brightly as two more customers entered the diner. Carlisle hadn't shown up the previous day either, and it was unlike him to skip his daily breakfast with us.

"Probably overslept," Grant offered as I filled the cup I set in front of him.

"Nope," Skip said without looking up at me.

"No?" I asked and set an empty coffee cup in front of him. I poured coffee into the cup and steam rose with the scent of freshly brewed coffee. "Don't tell me he's found another diner to hang out at?" I chuckled. Carlisle was one of my favorite customers. He would never leave Sam's. He was a dedicated regular.

Skip shook his head and picked up his cup. Before taking a sip, he looked at me, his eyes solemn. "He died."

I gasped. "Died? How? When? He was just here the day before yesterday."

"I heard from my brother Ralph that they pulled him from the Snake River last night." He took a sip of his coffee and looked down into the cup.

"The river? Are you serious? He's really gone?" I asked.

I was having trouble processing this information. I knew Skip was a year older than Carlisle because my mother had gone to school with Carlisle, Skip, and his brother Ralph. Carlisle and Ralph worked together at the county animal shelter while Skip worked at the feed store. Skip and Carlisle had been good friends, meeting at the diner nearly every morning. He wouldn't make up something like this.

He nodded again and looked up at me, his eyes showing his grief. "Yeah, he's gone. Doesn't make sense. I can't quite wrap my mind around it."

"That river's dangerous," Grant remarked somberly. "Too many people don't take heed of the signs out there telling people just how dangerous it is. Still, seems hard to believe Carlisle is gone."

I shook my head in disbelief. Carlisle had been a good guy. He was pleasant to talk to, whiling away the time between customers. "It's too cold to be out there swimming. Was he fishing?"

"Oh, he wasn't swimming. Carlisle couldn't swim. Had a fear of water. We took swimming lessons in the third grade, but he refused to get in the water past his knees," Skip said, looking at a spot on the counter just beyond his coffee cup.

Sam came out of the kitchen and looked at the two men at the counter. "How's everyone doing?"

"Carlisle drowned in the Snake River," I told him, looking at him sadly.

His eyes went big. "Wow. For real? That's terrible," he said, sounding shocked. "He was just here the day before yesterday."

I nodded as more customers came into the diner. When no one spoke for a minute, I put the carafe down. "I better tend to my tables."

Skip was gone before I was done taking the orders for my tables. I had wanted to talk to him before he left. I dropped the tickets off with Sam and headed back out to the front of the diner when Detective Cade Starkey walked in.

The detective was tall with chocolate brown hair and green eyes that made you take a second look. Not that I personally would take a second look. I was fresh off of a nasty divorce that left me without a book publisher and fired from the New York morning show where I did the cooking segments. That job had meant the world to me, and I hadn't recovered from losing it yet. My love life could wait.

"Good morning," I said to the detective. He wasn't one of my favorite people, considering he had suspected my mother and myself of murder earlier in the month. He was an odd one, with little sense of humor. He was also a stranger to Sparrow, having recently transferred from the Boise police department.

He nodded at me and headed to a chair at the counter. Carlisle's seat. "Good morning. Can I get a cup of coffee?"

I stared at him a moment as he sat down. Carlisle would never sit there again. I shook myself and nodded. Setting a cup down in front of him, I poured him some coffee from the carafe.

"Would you like to order some breakfast?" I asked.

"That cinnamon roll looks good," he said, nodding at the display case behind me.

I turned to get a plate and fork for him. "I heard there was a drowning in the Snake River last night," I said over my shoulder and removed a cinnamon roll from the display case.

"Yes, there was," he said and took a sip of his coffee. The detective takes it black.

When he didn't elaborate, I set the plate down in front of him.

"Carlisle was a nice guy," I said.

He looked up at me. "Does everyone around here know everyone else?"

I shrugged. "I suppose so. Small towns are like that." Sparrow, Idaho had a population of just over twenty thousand, and while I didn't know everyone, most faces were at least familiar.

He nodded and cut into his cinnamon roll with his fork. "I suppose they are."

"Skip Darlington was in here earlier and told me it was Carlisle," I supplied. I didn't want him to think I was out snooping, but I did want to know the details. Carlisle had been a good guy. He was someone that made me smile on my roughest days. "Carlisle and Skip were friends since grade school. It's hard on him, losing someone he was so close to."

"I suppose it would be," he said and looked up at me. "Did you know Carlisle well?"

"He came here for coffee and breakfast every morning. He rarely missed a day, and he always ordered a short stack of pancakes and coffee," I said. "I don't know why Carlisle would have been in that river. It's been so cold lately. And Skip said he couldn't swim."

The detective narrowed his eyes at me, and I immediately regretted sharing anything with him. All I needed was for him to take a close look at me. Silly to think so, but I felt like I should have kept my mouth shut.

"So what are you saying? That you think foul play was involved?"

"What? No, I have no idea if foul play was involved. I mean, I hardly know anything about Carlisle, other than he came here in the mornings and he was pleasant to talk to. My mother went to school with him and..." And that was when I stopped talking. My mother. I had been through enough with both of us being suspected of Celia Markson's murder, and here I was, throwing her name into the ring for yet another murder.

His eyes opened wide. "Your mother? How come her name gets thrown about every time someone dies around here?"

I gasped. "Now, you stop that. My mother's name is not being thrown around anywhere. You were wrong last time, you know."

He gave me a wicked grin. "You are excitable, aren't you?"

I put my hands on my hips. "I am not. Carlisle drowned, and I'm sorry to hear it. He'll be missed around here." With that, I turned and headed back out to the dining room. I had customers to attend to, and I didn't have time to stand around idly chatting. Georgia would be on me if I did. That one likes to point out everything wrong that I do.

Chapter Two

I GOT OFF WORK AT A few minutes past eleven. My feet ached, and I smelled like pancakes from working the morning shift. One good thing about working part-time at the diner—I got to go home early. My divorce hadn't left me with a lot of money, but it was enough that I only had to work part-time while working on my next cookbook. My ex-husband had been my publisher and had sabotaged my already published books and canceled all subsequent print runs. I hoped that by the time I finished the new book I was working on, he will have grown up and moved on. Otherwise, if this book tanked, I was going to have to look into serious full-time employment.

As I drove toward home, I took a detour to avoid roadwork. Sixth Street took me past a small tract of new homes being built where a shopping center had been torn down. The shopping center had long been an eyesore, and the community looked forward to the new homes being finished.

As I drove past the first house, I saw a red and white 1979 Ford Ranchero parked out front. That was when I remembered that Carlisle's wife, Margie Garlock, worked in construction. It may have been an unusual occupation for a woman, but Margie was an unusual woman. I pulled up behind the Ranchero and parked. The sound of nail guns and power tools filled the air when I opened my car door.

I spied Margie with a nail gun, working on the frame of one of the houses. She wore clear goggle-type safety glasses, a white hard hat that her pink-streaked hair peeked out from beneath, and brown lace-up boots. I headed over to her, hoping I wasn't breaking some safety rule by not wearing the same type of personal protective equipment that she and the other nearby workers wore.

I stopped about fifteen feet from her and waited for her to acknowledge me. After a moment, she looked over her shoulder and smiled at me.

"Hi Margie," I said as she shut off the nail gun.

"Hi, kiddo," she said, laying the power tool down and removing the leather gloves from her hands. Margie had called my twin sister Stormy and me kiddo ever since I could remember.

"I'm so sorry about Carlisle," I said when she walked over to me.

She nodded and looked away. "I don't think it's hit me yet, Rainey. Doesn't seem real."

"I can imagine," I said and wondered what she was doing here on the job. I didn't think I could have gone to work if my husband had just been found dead. "The diner won't be the same without him sitting in his seat at the front counter."

She nodded and took off her safety goggles. "Nothing's going to be the same without him. I don't know what I'll do with myself with him gone." Her voice cracked on the last part and my heart went out to her.

"I'm so sorry," I said. I wanted to reach out and hug her, but as friendly as Margie had always been, she wasn't a hugger. She was a lot larger than her husband had been, at nearly six-feet tall, and she probably outweighed him by fifty pounds. The weight appeared to be all muscle as evidenced by her muscled biceps revealed by the sleeveless t-shirt she wore.

She nodded again and looked into my eyes. "I don't know who would want to kill my Carlisle."

"What?" I gasped. "Someone murdered Carlisle?" Cade Starkey had seemed evasive earlier and I had just assumed Carlisle's death had been an accident.

She nodded. "That new detective said he had a head wound, most likely caused by someone hitting him over the head, and not from hitting a rock in the river. He did say there was a possibility he hit his head on a rock, but he didn't really think so."

"Wow," I said, trying to take this in. Carlisle had been so nice. Hearing that someone you knew had been murdered was shocking, to say the least.

"I will say, if it was an accident, I can't imagine what he was doing at the river. He couldn't swim and he never had any interest in fishing or anything else having to do with the river. I suppose he could have been killed somewhere else and taken to the river to make it look like an accident," she said thoughtfully.

"It does seem odd," I admitted. Ever since Skip had mentioned Carlisle not being able to swim, it had bothered me. "Skip Darlington said Carlisle was afraid of water. Is that true?"

She nodded. "Carlisle wasn't an outdoor fella. He liked to read and watch television. The only time he saw the great outdoors was when he took our dogs for a walk. Those dogs will miss him."

"When was the last time you saw him?" I hoped I didn't offend her with the question, but she seemed as puzzled as I was about his murder.

"Two nights ago," she said.

"Two nights ago? And they found him last night?" I asked. "You must have been worried when he didn't come home the first night." That was why Carlisle hadn't shown up at the diner. I felt a pang of guilt. I hadn't thought much of it when he didn't show up. Maybe if I would have asked someone...

"No, he went to see his mother over in Freely early Monday evening. She hasn't been feeling well, so I didn't realize something wasn't right. It was late last night when they found him and I haven't even told her yet. It'll kill her. She loved her son like all good mamas do. I suppose I'll have to drive over there tonight and tell her." She shook her head and looked over at the house she had been working on.

I nodded, a little surprised to hear Carlisle's mother hadn't been told yet. It would be a shock and I felt terrible for her.

"Margie, why are you here at work?" I asked gently. "Wouldn't you feel better at home?"

She turned back to me and gave me a weak smile. "It makes me feel better to be doing something. Like I said, I'm putting off talking to Carlisle's mother and our house just feels empty now."

"I understand. If there's anything my mother or I can do for you, you'll let us know, won't you? Anything at all."

She nodded. "That sure is nice of you, Stormy."

I smiled but didn't correct her. The grief must have been confusing her.

"I mean it, Margie. If we can do anything at all for you, don't hesitate to call," I said.

She looked at me, her eyebrows furrowed. "You want to know something? If someone did hurt my Carlisle, I'd say it was Gary Dunning."

"Gary Dunning? Doesn't he work at the shelter with Carlisle?"

She nodded. "Gary hated Carlisle. Carlisle would come home from work frustrated because Gary would always try to trip him up. He'd sabotage his work and try to turn his coworkers against him."

I didn't know Gary well at all, but a couple of years earlier when my mother adopted her cat, Poofy, he had been the one to assist us. He seemed like an okay guy.

"Did you mention it to the detective?"

She nodded. "Oh yeah, I did. He said he would look into it. When Carlisle applied for the supervisor position at the shelter, Gary applied for it, too. Ever since Carlisle got the job, Gary's had it in for him."

"That's awful," I said. "I'm sure the detective will talk to him."

"Hey," a voice said, and we both looked over as Mark Price approached. He nodded at me. "How are things going?"

I smiled. When people couldn't tell whether they were talking to my identical twin sister, or me they tended to leave out using a name. I guess they don't want to feel awkward about getting it wrong, but not using at least one of our names made for its own awkwardness.

"I'm doing okay, Mark," I said. "I just stopped to see how Margie was doing. I heard about Carlisle at the Diner. He stopped in for breakfast every weekday morning. He'll be missed."

His face fell, and he glanced at Margie and then returned his eyes to mine. "Yeah. That's a terrible thing. I don't know how it happened." Mark was about Margie's age and had black hair and a slight potbelly. He looked perpetually in need of a shave.

"Makes you wonder what he was doing out at the river, doesn't it?" I asked.

He looked at the house Margie had been working on and then glanced at Margie, then back to me. "I know that detective said it was probably a murder, but I have to wonder about that. Carlisle was a good guy. Maybe he went fishing or something. You never know. Or maybe he was hunting down a stray animal out there. That could be it."

He looked hopeful on the last part, but it made me feel funny. He almost seemed to prefer it if it was found that Carlisle had had an accident. Something scratched at the back of my mind that I couldn't quite remember about him.

"I suppose that could be," I said, agreeing with him. "That could have been the reason he was out there."

Carlisle had worked for the county for years and had been almost single-handedly responsible for helping our county animal shelter achieve the status of a no-kill shelter. A fact that everyone I knew was proud of. It wouldn't surprise me at all if he had been out at the river for that very reason.

"Well, we better get back to work," Mark said, looking at Margie.

She nodded. "Yeah, our supervisor has been on us to get the framework on this house done before the end of the week."

"Well, I don't want to keep you then," I said. "And don't forget, if you need anything, let me know, Margie."

"Thanks, Rainey," she said, and they both turned back to the house. She picked up her nail gun and got to work on the house frame again.

I looked over the house they were working on. The house would be a modest-sized ranch. I had seen the plans online and if the cookbook did as well as I hoped, maybe I'd be able to put a down payment on one of these houses and move out of my mother's house. It was great living with my mother, but I was thirty-five and the days of being dependent on her were long over. At least, I hoped they were.

I turned and headed back to my car. Once inside and buckled in, I started my car and looked back at Mark. Then I remembered my mother had told me he lived in a trailer on Margie and Carlisle's property. Mark was the same age as my mother and they had all gone to school together.

I looked over my shoulder and pulled away from the curb. Had Mark seemed nervous when talking about Carlisle or was he just grieving an old friend?

Chapter Three

"I CAN HARDLY BELIEVE poor Carlisle is dead," Mom said, stirring sugar into her glass of tea. "I just talked to him last week. Said he was going to buy a new barbeque down at the hardware store. They're having a twenty percent off sale."

"It seems weird to see his chair empty at the diner counter," I agreed and squeezed another lemon over the stainless steel strainer. I was experimenting with a lemon chiffon pie. When I had started working on recipes for my new cookbook, I wasn't sure of a theme. The past few days I was pretty sure I was going with an Americana theme. I wanted each recipe to feel like it could have come out of any American housewife's kitchen somewhere in the past five to eight decades.

"Poor Margie," Stormy said, and took a sip of her tea. "I can't imagine."

"Can I have some pie?" Bonney asked. Bonney was Stormy's seven-year-old daughter. She was the apple of my eye and if we had been the same age, she could have been my twin. Sure, Stormy and I were identical twins so it shouldn't be a surprise that Bonney and I looked so much alike, but there was more to it than that. The girl was so much like me she could sometimes finish my sentences.

"You'll get the first piece, Bonney," I promised her.

I carefully measured out the sugar and poured it into the saucepan on the stove, adding the lemon juice to it.

"Mom, didn't you go to school with Carlisle?" Stormy asked. She had her blond hair tied up with a twisted red bandana and looked pretty cute. I was going to have to try that look.

Mom nodded. "I did. He had the hots for me in ninth grade, but he was a skinny pipsqueak. I put him off, hoping your dad would ask me out. He did, and I turned Carlisle down."

"No sense in being upfront with him, eh?" I needled.

She snorted. "I was fourteen. I might not have had my ethics firmly in place at that age."

"It's funny that he was down by the river to begin with, let alone in it," I said. "Skip Darlington said he couldn't swim and didn't like water."

"That's true," Mom said thoughtfully. "He would never join us when we had parties at the river during the summer while we were in high school."

"I wonder what he was doing there, then," Stormy said. "If he didn't like water, it doesn't seem like he would be there hanging out."

"Mark Price wondered if he might have been down there to catch a stray dog," I said, turning the heat on beneath the pan. The smell of lemons filled the kitchen and my mouth watered, thinking about the pie.

"Could be," Mom said. "That Carlisle sure was a nice guy."

"I heard something," Stormy said. When I turned to look at her, her eyes cut to Bonney. "Bonney, why don't you go into the living room and watch TV? It will be awhile before Aunt Rainey is done with the pie."

Bonney sighed. "Okay, Mom. Aunt Rainey, don't forget I get the first piece."

I smiled. "No problem, sweetheart. You'll get the first piece."

When Bonney was safely out of the room and the television turned on, I turned to Stormy with a raised eyebrow.

"I heard Margie was seeing someone," she whispered.

Mom let out a titter. "Oh, come on, Stormy. Not Margie. She's, well, she's Margie."

"Mom, that's not very nice," I said. Margie did have the build of a construction worker, but after all, that's what she was. But she didn't seem to be the sort of person that would cheat.

Mom shrugged. "I don't mean to be unkind, but she has a rough personality to match her rough exterior. Carlisle was the sensitive one in the relationship. Romance doesn't seem to be her forte."

I turned back to the saucepan and stirred the lemon juice and sugar. It was true about Carlisle. He seemed like the sweetest person around and that made his death that much harder.

"Stormy, will you keep an eye on the lemon and sugar? I'm going to work on the crust."

I switched places with Stormy at the kitchen island and got to work measuring out the flour for the piecrust. Mom had renovated an old Victorian house, adding in a lot of old historic touches, but there were certain things she had added that were distinctly modern, like the kitchen island and the dishwasher.

"I don't think Margie has it in her to cheat on Carlisle," Mom murmured. "But if she did, I'd think it was with Mark Price. They're together all the time."

I shot her a look. "Does he still live on their property in his trailer?"

She nodded and picked up the recipe card I had been making notes on. "As far as I know, he does. Are you sure you're putting enough sugar in this?"

"We'll have to wait and see if it's enough." I didn't want to think about Margie cheating. "Mark living there doesn't mean a thing," I said and began cutting cold butter into the flour and salt mixture. And it really didn't mean anything, did it? Surely Margie wouldn't move her boyfriend onto the property she shared with her husband, would she? I had always thought of Margie as a nice person and I couldn't see her doing that.

"Nope, not a thing," Mom said without looking at me.

"Do you think it was foul play? I mean, how would anyone know? If someone pushed him into the river and he couldn't swim, he'd drown and who would know that's what happened? Those currents can get pretty swift," Stormy said.

"I might know something. And maybe I shouldn't say anything," I said, gently working the piecrust dough. I didn't want to overdo it and make it tough.

"And?" Mom asked when I didn't continue.

"I don't know," I said, feeling like I shouldn't say anything. Maybe I should keep some things to myself.

"Okay, you can't bring something up and then hold out on us," Stormy said, stirring the lemon juice and sugar. "What do you know?"

"Maybe I shouldn't say it. There was some wind and rain last night, anyway. Maybe the banks of the river just got muddy, and he slipped."

"Spill it," Mom said.

I sighed. "Margie said the detective told her Carlisle was murdered. He had a head wound. But when the detective came into the diner and I brought up the fact that Carlisle had drowned, he seemed almost evasive."

"Murder?" Mom said. "I can't imagine who would kill Carlisle."

"Me either," Stormy said. "But I can see where the detective wouldn't want to tell you anything. If it's a murder, the police are going to investigate."

"And that's why we need to keep this to ourselves. We don't need everyone in town talking about it," I pointed out. I looked at both of them. "Promise me."

They both nodded their agreement as I pressed the piecrust into the glass pie pan. We were silent for a couple of minutes while I crimped the edges of the piecrust.

"Did I tell you that Natalie has definitely decided on UCLA?" Stormy asked, changing the subject. "It seems like such a big school and Los Angeles is so dangerous and so far away. I told Bob she shouldn't go."

Poor Stormy was about to face the fact that her eldest child was going off to college in the fall. She had dug her heels in for months, trying to persuade Natalie to stay in Idaho. Natalie dug her own heels in and even though Stormy had been hoping Natalie would change her mind and go to a local college, it wasn't going to happen.

"Natalie is a bright, mature girl," I pointed out. "She's going to be fantastically successful at whatever she does. You and Bob did a great job raising her."

"Rainey is right, Stormy. Natalie can handle it," Mom said gently. "She's a smart girl."

Stormy sighed. "I was hoping for a little more support from the two of you. It would be so much better if she at least stayed in Idaho."

"You have our support in everything," I said, satisfied with the piecrust. "But you've got to let Natalie fly the nest. She's ready."

She looked at me with tears in her eyes and nodded. "I guess you're right."

Stormy had five children. Natalie was seventeen, Brent was fourteen, Curtis was thirteen, Bonney was seven and Lizzy was four. They were all wonderful kids, and I had no doubts about where they were headed in life. They were on the road to success. I may have been a little biased, but I was allowed to be. I was their favorite, and only, aunt.

"Don't worry about it," Mom said. "And besides. You're only thirty-five. You can have another baby and replace her if things don't work out."

I groaned. Mom and her smart remarks.

"Thanks, Mom, but I'm attached to this one. And I already told Bob the baby factory was closed, although he'd love to have five more. It's Rainey's turn," Stormy said, eyeing me.

"Oh no, don't you start that. If I have a kid, that's great, but I'm not in the market for one."

I had wanted a baby as soon as my ex-husband and I had gotten married. He had waited until after the wedding to spring on me the fact that he never wanted a baby. Ever. I should have known that was the case, considering he avoided the subject when I brought it up while we were dating. I quickly learned to not bring it up. I just assumed he wasn't ready because we weren't married yet. And then he told me the truth. On our honeymoon. In the end, I was glad we hadn't had any. He cheated, and that was the end of us. Dragging a kid through a divorce was the last thing I wanted to do, especially considering how nasty the divorce had turned out. But, maybe someday I would get that soft, sweet-smelling bundle of joy. Until then, I would enjoy my sister's kids.

Chapter Four

I PUSHED OPEN THE DINER door and my eyes immediately went to the corner seat where Carlisle normally sat. My heart dropped, and a lump came to my throat. He was a good guy. I would miss him.

"Good morning, Rainey," Detective Cade Starkey said. He sat at the far end of the counter and he let his eyes roam to the same empty chair mine had gone to. "How are you this morning?"

The detective was beginning to make it a habit to eat at Sam's Diner. It both annoyed me and made me a little happy to see him. I shrugged off the feeling and took a deep breath, turning toward him before heading to the back to stow my purse and find a clean apron.

"I'm doing fine. Well, as fine as can be expected, I guess."

He nodded. "It's a shame when someone nice is killed."

My antenna went up. "Killed? So it wasn't an accident?" Was he going to admit he knew more than he had let on the previous day?

"Well," he said with a slight pause. "We don't know everything we need to know to make a final determination about Carlisle's death, but there was blunt force trauma to his head. Maybe it would be more correct to have said 'it's a shame when someone nice dies'. We just don't know for sure what happened yet."

I narrowed my eyes in thought. "So, it could have been from an accident? Like if he was in a boat and slipped and fell into the water? And maybe the head trauma was from hitting a rock?" I moved over closer to him so the customers in the diner couldn't hear our conversation.

"It's certainly a possibility, although no boats have been found in the river. But it could have been washed down river. The medical examiner is going to conduct an autopsy and we'll know more then," he said and took a drink of his coffee.

I took the liberty of sitting on the stool next to him. His plate of scrambled eggs, bacon, and toast made my stomach growl. I had left the house without eating breakfast again.

"Carlisle really was a nice guy. I'm not sure that we can conclude it was a murder," I said thoughtfully. "I can't imagine anyone wanting him dead."

He chuckled. "I don't think we're coming to conclusions at this point. And lots of really nice people get killed so that's not really reason enough to conclude that he wasn't murdered. But like I said, I should have used the word 'dies'. My apologies."

I looked into his dark green eyes for a moment. That chocolate brown hair of his was shining in the morning light that was streaming through the diner window and I could smell a hint of his cologne. It was disconcerting, to say the least.

"I'll ask around and see if anyone knows anything," I said. "Maybe someone will tell me something they wouldn't tell the police."

"Oh, wait a minute now," he said sitting up straighter. "A police investigation is no place for you. Let the police handle this."

I looked at him. "What? I can help you find out information. You're practically a stranger here to Sparrow and people won't trust you enough to talk to you."

He chuckled again. "Listen, Rainey, I've been a detective for fifteen years. I've got this. Don't you worry yourself about Carlisle's death. If it is a murder, you might be getting yourself into trouble and no one wants that."

"Don't you worry about me, Mr. Detective," I said confidently and stood up. "I know what I'm doing."

I was feeling overly confident. I had caught a killer before. Well, sort of. Actually, the killer had come to me, but I had defended myself quite well when I was attacked and I was feeling my oats, as my mother liked to say.

He sighed loudly. "Rainey. Stay out of this. It's none of your business. Don't make me resort to giving you an official warning. I might have to take you to jail if you interfere with the investigation."

I narrowed my eyes at him, and brushed a loose strand of my blond hair out of my eyes. I needed a haircut and a brightening up of my color. "Fine. I'll mind my own business."

If my hands had been free, I would have had my fingers crossed, but I was holding a cup of coffee in one hand and I had switched my purse to the other. It irritated me that he had told me to stay out of the investigation, but I wasn't going to let on. It was none of his business what I did.

"I mean it," he warned as I turned and headed toward the break room.

"Got it," I said over my shoulder.

"I hope you do," he warned.

"Good morning Sam," I called as I headed to put my purse up.

MY FEET ACHED AS I drove home. I loved the people I worked with, well most of them, but waitressing was hard work. There was no way to get around that. I still missed being on the morning television program, cooking and creating beautiful food. Maybe one day I wouldn't miss it so much, but for now, I did. My creativity had been squashed when my ex-husband had tried to sabotage my career. Actually, he had more than tried. He had done it.

I turned my car into the Savemore convenience store. I needed gas and a soda. My mouth was parched, and I hadn't had a soft drink in what seemed like forever.

I pulled up to the gas pumps, parked my car, and turned the engine off. There was an old beat up red Ford pickup that had pulled up to the pump in front of me. Mark Price got out of the truck at the same time I got out of my car.

"Hi, Mark," I said.

"Hi," he said, and again looked like he was unsure of whether he was speaking to my sister or me. "How are you?"

"Tired. I just got off work. How about you?"

"Me too. I'm looking forward to going home and kicking my boots off," he said and went to the pump to run his card through the card reader. I did the same on my pump and selected the grade of gas I needed.

Before I could get to my gas tank, Mark had sidled up to me. "Stormy, can I tell you something?"

I nodded. "It's Rainey. Sure."

"Oh, sorry, Rainey. I hate to say it, but I have a feeling Margie knows more about Carlisle's death than she's letting on." He leaned against the back of my car and spoke in low tones.

I was surprised to hear this. "What do you mean?"

"I hate to say it," he repeated. "You know both Margie and Carlisle have done a lot for me. When my wife left me two years ago, I was homeless. I hate to talk about it, but I was. I was sleeping on friends' couches. Sometimes I was sleeping out behind the old shopping center that used to be where the new houses we're building are now. Carlisle invited me to live in their old trailer on their property. I jumped at the chance. I really appreciate that. But, Carlisle and Margie argued. A lot."

I stared at him, taking this in. My mind refused to believe that Margie could kill anyone, but I wondered how well I actually knew her.

"Just because people fight doesn't mean they would kill each other," I pointed out.

"I know, I know," he said and looked over his shoulder. "Look, I guess I could be wrong, but one night they were going at it and I heard her say she would kill him if he didn't stop. I don't know what it was that she wanted him to stop, but she was mad."

I nodded, trying to process this. Did Cade Starkey know Carlisle and Margie fought? I didn't know and I wasn't sure I wanted to tell him. He had already told me to stay out of the investigation, but this seemed like important information.

"I have a hard time believing Margie could have killed Carlisle. She loved him," I said. "Where is she now?"

"She went to Freely to tell Carlisle's mother that he's dead. She said she'd be there a couple of days."

"Poor thing," I said, thinking about his mother. I had met her on several occasions when Carlisle had brought her into the diner for lunch when she visited. "I can't imagine having your child die."

He nodded. "Carlisle was her only child. It's got to be rough."

"Oh, no," I said. "That kind of makes it worse."

He nodded. "Yeah. Margie said she'd be back tomorrow or the next day. I guess I could be wrong about her, but I have a sneaking suspicion."

"I hope you're wrong," I said, leaning against my car.

He was quiet a moment. "You know, the more I think about it, the more I think I'm probably wrong," he said. His face had gone pale. "Hey, don't tell anyone I said that about Margie, okay? I don't want her getting mad at me. I need to stay in that trailer. I'm still paying alimony and I can't afford another place to stay. Not to mention the fact that I don't want someone like her mad at me."

"No, of course not. I wouldn't spread that around," I assured him. "I'm sure the police will find the real killer."

He nodded again. "I'm sure you're right. Well, I better get my gas and get going." He turned and went back to his truck and removed the gas cap.

I put the gas nozzle into my gas tank and leaned against my car again. There went the theory that Mark and Margie were having an affair. He wouldn't volunteer the fact that he wondered if she had killed her husband if they were an item.

Chapter Five

I PICKED UP MY GYM bag from the passenger seat and got out of my car. I had taken kickboxing classes when I lived in New York as a means of self-defense. It came in handy when you needed to kick someone hard enough to stop them in their tracks. It would have been nice to say I had never had the need to do that, but I had.

I pushed open the door to the gym and looked around. It was late afternoon, so there were only five other people working out on the machines. I didn't have a class, but I wanted to get in a workout with the heavy bags. It kept me sharp.

My mind was working overtime as I headed to the lockers to stow my bag, mulling over the things that I had heard about Carlisle's death. As much as I hated to say it, I thought Margie might be a prime suspect. The obvious reason was that Margie was so much bigger than Carlisle. It wouldn't have taken much for her to hit him over the head with one of those power tools she owned. All she would have had to do after that was drag his body to the river and dump it.

But did she have a motive? I thought she and Mark might be having an affair, but he had pointed his finger at her. That wasn't much of a relationship if he was so ready to say she may have killed her husband. But if she and Carlisle were fighting as regularly and viciously as Mark indicated, then maybe she had just lost her temper one night and hit him with something. She may not have even meant to kill him. If that were the case, would she have told me Detective Starkey said Carlisle was murdered? It seemed like she would want to keep that sort of thing quiet out of guilt.

I changed into my workout clothes in the locker room, pulled my hair back into a ponytail, and headed out to the gym floor. My gloves were hot pink and cute as could be. I went straight to the bags, did a quick warm up and then began punching and kicking. The bags were in the corner and I had them to myself. I got in a few good kicks and then caught someone approach out of the corner of my eye.

"Well, I'd hate to be on the business end of one of those kicks," Cade Starkey said with a grin.

I froze, staring at him. He was dressed in black workout shorts and a white tee. He looked like he worked out regularly, not that I noticed things like that.

"What are you doing here? Aren't you supposed to be at work?" I asked, relaxing my stance.

He grinned. "Most days I am at work this time of day, yes. But I've been putting in a lot of late hours the past few days, so I decided to knock off early and get a workout in. It helps blow off steam."

"Investigating Carlisle's murder keeping you busy?" I asked, putting one gloved hand on the heavy bag.

"All murders keep you busy. But, we still don't know for certain that it's a murder," he said, putting one hand on the other heavy punching bag.

"It is a murder, isn't it?" I asked. "I know you don't want to give away any of the details, but I think from what you told me yesterday, you know the truth. Besides that, people are already talking."

He sighed, keeping his eyes on me. "Looks like it is," he admitted. "News travels fast in this town."

"It does. How do you know he didn't just hit his head on some rocks?" I asked. "Those currents are fast out there." It seemed to me that it would be hard to tell blunt force trauma from hitting his head on a rock.

"Location and size of the wound would make it all wrong. Even though the currents are swift in the Snake River, this was some really major trauma. Of course, we may find out differently after the autopsy results come back, but for now, we're treating it as a murder. Why? Do you have any ideas about who may have done it?" He moved closer and leaned on another bag, holding it steady with one hand.

I wasn't sure if he was teasing me or if he really wanted to hear my thoughts on the subject. I decided to bite. "If I had to guess, I might pick his wife. Although, when I first heard about it, I didn't think it was possible for her to have done it. She doesn't seem the type."

"What made you change your mind?" he asked.

I shrugged. "I guess I've heard a few things." I reached back and tightened my ponytail holder and looked him in the eye.

"Are you going to enlighten me?" he asked with a smirk.

I sighed. "Mark Price said Margie and Carlisle argued. A lot. I guess they were loud, and he thought it was pretty serious. He thought she might have killed Carlisle. I wouldn't have thought they had marital problems if Mark hadn't said it. Carlisle always spoke so well of Margie."

"Lots of people argue, but I suppose it's good to keep in mind. Margie said Mark lives on their property?"

I nodded. "In an old trailer. I hate to blame Margie. I hope she didn't do it. She's kind of what some people might consider rough in her mannerisms, but she's got a good heart." I felt incredibly guilty talking about Margie this way. I hoped it turned out to be someone else. And if she didn't do it, I'd feel even guiltier for talking about her this way.

"What did they argue about?" he asked. "Did Mark say?"

I shook my head and waited for a man that was walking by to move out of earshot.

"He didn't say. I had heard Mark and Margie were seeing each other on the side. I can't see how that could be true if he was willing to say he thought Margie had something to do with Carlisle's death," I said.

He considered this a moment, then he looked at me. "Tell me, Ms. Daye. Why are you interested in this case? It seems like you know an awful lot about it."

I suppressed the desire to roll my eyes. I should have known better than to say anything and kept my mouth shut.

"I'm not interested. I mean, I'm interested from the standpoint that Margie and Carlisle are nice people. I feel bad about what happened. Carlisle was a really nice guy and I just want to see justice done for him."

I hoped he wouldn't think I had something to do with this. I had had enough of being a suspect in a murder investigation. I didn't need the headache.

"I appreciate the information, however, I'm going to have to insist once again that you stay out of this. You seem to be a little too curious about things like this," he said. The smirk was back. "We've already talked about this, remember?"

I didn't know if he thought he was funny, but I didn't appreciate the insinuation that I had anything to do with Carlisle's death.

"Listen, I am not too curious about anything. I am also not sticking my nose into anything. I am just concerned that we have a murderer on the loose and someone I consider a friend, even if he wasn't a close friend, was murdered," I said, talking much faster than I intended. "You need to find the killer."

He put both hands up, palms toward me. "All right, calm down. We'll find the killer. Just keep yourself out of trouble, okay?"

I gasped. This man could make my blood boil!

"Detective Starkey, I assure you I am calm. I can also assure you that I will stay safe. Just do me and the rest of Sparrow a favor and get Carlisle's killer off the street."

I turned away from him and began punching the bag. Cade Starkey was annoying and condescending and I had nothing more to say to him.

He chuckled and took a step away from the bag he was leaning on.

"Okay, okay. Message received. I promise to find the killer as soon as possible. Just don't get involved. I don't want you or anyone else hurt."

I ignored him and kept punching the bag, wishing it was his face. No, that's not true. I would never hit anyone unless it was in self-defense, but his attitude was getting me charged up.

But at least it gave me a good workout.

He chuckled again when I didn't say anything else and walked away. Some people were infuriating. I just couldn't tell if he was doing it on purpose or if annoying me just came naturally to him. The thing that made me angriest about his attitude was the fact that he was so darned attractive.

Chapter Six

I WAS OFF WORK THE next day and after lying around in my pajamas for far longer than any self-respecting person should do; I headed over to the British Tea and Coffee Company. The shop was owned by Agatha Broome, an English woman who was one of the sweetest people I knew.

"Hi Agatha," I called when I spotted her stocking the candy shelves. Agatha carried all sorts of British delectables in candy, cookies, and other assorted sweets. It was fun just to stand and look at what was on the shelves. It made me long for a country I had never visited.

"Hello, Sweetheart," she said, nodding. "I've brought in some more Cadbury chocolates. The real Cadbury, you know."

I went to her and looked at the candy bars she was putting out on the shelves. The scent of chocolate filled the area, and I inhaled deeply.

"This is the stuff of heaven. I think chocolate is my very favorite thing in the whole world."

"Mine, too. As long as I allow myself one small piece, I can keep things under control. If I allow myself one bite more, I have to eat everything I can get my hands on."

I chuckled. "Me, too. One day though, I'd like to just sit and eat to my heart's content."

"You and me both," she said. Then she became serious. "Did you hear what happened to poor Carlisle Garlock?"

"I did, it's terrible. He came into the diner every morning and ordered a short stack of pancakes and a black coffee. I'll miss him," I said, brushing my hair back from my face.

She nodded. "He stopped in here at least a couple times a week. He was a nice fellow. I shall miss him. His wife came in this morning. Poor thing. She said she had no idea what he was doing at the river."

"She's back in town?"

She shrugged. "I didn't know she left."

"Mark Price said she had gone to Freely to tell Carlisle's mother what happened. I suppose she didn't stay long."

I moved over to the front counter to order a large peppermint mocha. It may not have been Christmas, but it sounded good to me. It was the first of June and the weather was starting to warm up, but I didn't care. Hot coffee is always in style. Agatha followed me over to make my drink.

She looked at me as she poured the coffee. "The poor thing. Losing a child at any age is awful."

Agatha said it like she knew this firsthand. She had never mentioned children and I suppose I had assumed she had children and they still lived in England.

"It really is," I said as she rang up my order. "Agatha, have you heard anything else? About Carlisle or Margie?"

She looked over her shoulder at her assistant who was making a frozen coffee for another customer. She put a finger to her lips and nodded.

"Let's have a seat, shall we?" she said and picked up a cup of tea she had made for herself earlier.

I paid for my coffee and then we headed for a table. I sat across from her and waited for her to get comfortable.

"I heard Carlisle and his coworker Gary Dunning didn't get along. Seems they both wanted the same job and when Carlisle got it, Gary never treated him the same after that," she said and took a sip of her cup of tea.

"How do you know this?" I asked.

"Do you know Brenda Fields? She works in the office at the shelter. She said things were very tense between the two of them after Carlisle got the promotion," she said, lowering her voice and looking over her shoulder again.

I nodded. "Margie mentioned he had trouble with Gary."

"Carlisle did a great job at the shelter. You already know that it was because of him that the county now has a no-kill shelter. He had a good heart," she said sadly and stirred her tea.

"He was so proud of the work he did at the shelter," I said, remembering when he had told me about the no-kill status. I had just moved back to town and gotten the job at the diner. He beamed when he spoke of it.

"We're all proud of him for that," Agatha agreed.

I glanced up and saw the detective enter the shop and I scowled. I couldn't help it. He was turning up everywhere it seemed.

"What's the matter?" Agatha asked, noting my scowl. "That's a fine detective Sparrow has there. And handsome, too."

"He may be handsome, but he's annoying and a smart aleck, and—and, I don't know," I said, becoming flustered.

Agatha giggled. "Oh, deary, I do think that sounds like you might be attracted to him."

I gasped, glanced at the detective's back as he got in line and then looked back at Agatha. "That is not true. I do not like him at all."

Agatha looked at me with a grin that said she didn't believe a word of it and that made me more flustered.

"Are you sure you don't like him?" she asked.

I shook my head. "No. Not even a little bit." I put my cup to my lips so I wouldn't have to say anything more.

"Okay, then," she said and looked down into her tea before taking another sip. She couldn't hide her grin behind the cup though.

I put my cup down. "It's a beautiful day out," I said changing the subject.

Agatha raised an eyebrow at me. "Indeed it is."

When Cade paid for his drink, he sat at the table nearest to our table. I glance at Agatha and she grinned. I shook my head. She was incorrigible.

He looked over at us. "How are you ladies this afternoon?"

"We're fine, Detective," Agatha said, still smiling. "Anything new on the murder?"

His eyes went to mine, and I looked away. "News sure does travel quickly around here."

"Indeed it does," Agatha said. "Small towns are like that, both here and in England. I suspect they're the same the world over. News travels fast whether it's good or bad. Doesn't seem to matter."

"Indeed," he said. "I just hope people don't think they can stick their noses into things and get carried away with asking questions about it."

I sighed loudly. "If some people do want to stick their noses into it, I can't imagine there would be anything you could do about it."

"I bet I might be able to. That is if they actually take any kind of action and get in the way. Say, obstruction of justice?"

I rolled my eyes. "You are so full of yourself. No one is sticking their nose into anything and no one wants to obstruct justice. Why don't you let it go?"

Agatha's eyes danced with merriment and I looked down at my coffee. I was doing exactly what she had said I was doing-becoming interested in the detective even if it wasn't in a positive way.

"You do get excited, don't you?" he said with a smirk.

I clenched my teeth and took a drink of my coffee.

"Now, detective, you won't find finer people in the whole state of Idaho than the Dayes. They're all kind and wonderful, not to mention pretty as a picture," Agatha said.

I knew she was trying to help, but this just made me more embarrassed. I needed to end my misery, so I got to my feet.

"I've got to get going. I've got errands to run," I said. "I'll talk to you later, Agatha." I didn't acknowledge the detective and headed for the door amid Agatha's giggles.

It was probably immature to leave like that but I didn't care. I couldn't understand why I behaved the way I did around the detective. I needed to get out into the sun and get some fresh air. That would clear my head.

Chapter Seven

"I CAN'T TELL YOU HOW much I appreciate this," Stormy said, dropping Bonney's backpack onto the sofa. "I promise I won't be late to pick them up."

"It's no problem," I said. "I don't have to go to work until 11:00. Mom said I could drop them off at the flower shop on my way to work."

"Thanks, you guys are the best!" she said and hurried out the door.

"So, have you two had breakfast?" I asked Lizzy and Bonney. Stormy had called at the last minute with an emergency trip to take her son Brent to the doctor. Everyone in the household had come down with the flu. Button and Lizzy had gotten it first and were nearly recovered now.

"Yes, we had cereal," Bonney said. "I wanted *Lucky Charms*, but my mom said I had to eat *Cheerios*."

"*Cheerios* are good," I said.

"I want to go to daycare," Lizzy said, sitting next to her backpack and unzipping it. "It's share day. I brought my pony. See?" She held up a pink pony that had a yellow mane and tail.

"That pony is adorable, Lizzy, but your mom wants you to wait one more day before going back." It was the beginning of June and school ended in three days for Bonney. If it were up to me, I would have just kept her home instead of sending her for the last three days. But then, I only had aunt responsibilities where the kids were concerned and not mom responsibilities, so there's that.

She sighed. "Okay, fine. One more day. But I'll miss share day."

"There's always next week, honey," I assured her. Lizzy loved daycare and would continue to go throughout the summer. There would be another share day for her to bring the pony.

"I don't mind missing school," Bonney said.

I smiled. "I wouldn't either. How are you two feeling today?"

"We're fine, Auntie Rainey. We don't feel sick at all," she said, sitting on the ottoman. "Can we watch TV?"

"Sure," I said. I picked up the remote and turned the television on to the Disney channel.

The truth was, I had wanted to stop by the animal shelter and see if Gary was around before I went to work. Did I expect him to confess to Carlisle's murder? Nope. But you never knew what you could find out just in casual conversation. Cade Starkey may have wanted me to stay out of things, but I was just stubborn enough to stick my nose where it didn't belong.

"Hey, if you two are really feeling okay, how about we go for a little drive?" I suggested, placing my hand on Lizzy's forehead just to make sure she wasn't sick. It was as cool as could be, so I reached over and checked Bonney's. Ditto. I didn't think

Stormy would be too upset if I took them for a drive. They had eaten breakfast, and they seemed to feel fine.

"Yeah!" Lizzy said. "Can I bring my pony?"

"Sure you can," I said and headed to my room to get my purse.

"Where are we going?" Bonney called after me.

"We're going to go look at puppies and kitties at the shelter. But I have to warn you that we probably can't pet them. We'll just look," I said when I came back into the room.

"I wanna pet them," Lizzy said.

"Are you going to get a puppy?" Bonney asked me. "We could come and visit it and help you take care of it."

"We'll see, sweetie," I said, and we headed out the door. "But today we'll just look at them."

WE ARRIVED AT THE SHELTER just as they were opening. "Hi, I said to the woman at the front desk. Can we take a look at the animals?"

"Sure," she said. "You can go on back. There are some attendants back there, so if you need any help, they'll assist you."

"Great, thanks," I said and led the way to the big swinging doors that separated the animal enclosures from the front office.

The animals were kept in kennels and cages with cats on one side and dogs on the other. The dogs started barking and jockeying for position as we approached the kennels.

"Awe, look at the puppies," Bonney said as we approached a kennel with an assortment of puppies in it.

"I want one!" Lizzy squealed.

That was when I realized my mistake. The girls were going to have a hard time leaving the animals behind when we left. And so was I, I realized when a little black puppy started whining and crying, his big brown eyes pleading with me to take him home. I squatted down and stuck my fingers through the chain link kennel gate and was rewarded with frantic licking.

"They're so cute," I said.

"Do you think we can get one?" Bonney asked, sticking her fingers through the gate to pet a white and black spotted puppy.

"I think what we should do is take a look and then tell your mom about them," I said. I was putting the responsibility of saying no onto my sister. It wasn't right, but I hadn't thought this through. The girls were going to want to bring a puppy home.

"More Puppies!" Lizzy squealed when she looked into the next kennel.

"Can I help you, folks?" I heard someone from behind me say.

I stood up and turned around, coming face to face with Gary Dunning.

"Hi Stormy," he said, glancing at the girls.

"It's Rainey," I said. "I've got kid duty this morning."

He chuckled. "I see. So are you all going to pick out a puppy today?"

"Well," I said and looked at the kennel of puppies. "I'm not sure if it will be today. You know, when I was a kid we had a red dachshund puppy that was the best dog in the whole world. I have always wanted to get another one."

"Dachshunds are good little dogs," he said, nodding. "But as soon as they come in, someone adopts them. They're very popular."

"I kind of thought that might be the case," I said. "Maybe one day I'll find another one."

"I'll keep you in mind if we get one in," he said. "Like I said, they go fast, but I can put it aside for a day or so."

I smiled. "That would be great. Hey, Gary, how are you doing? I heard about Carlisle. I can only imagine how much you all miss him around here."

The smile left his face. "It's a tragedy. This place won't be the same without him. He was instrumental in making this place run as smoothly as it does. But I'm sure you already know that with the newspaper articles and the news coming out to do a segment on the fact that we're a no-kill shelter now."

"That was such an awesome thing he did for this county and the animals," I agreed. "The mayor said our shelter would be the model for all the other shelters in the state."

He nodded and looked away. "He'll be missed."

"It's such a tragedy."

He nodded again and looked back at me. "I don't know what he was doing down at the river. He hated the water. It doesn't make sense."

"I heard Carlisle was murdered," I said, whispering the word 'murder'. The girls had moved over to the next kennel, giggling and laughing as the dogs licked their fingers and not paying any attention to our conversation.

His eyes went wide. "Murdered? I hadn't heard that," he said thoughtfully. "Are you sure?"

"His wife said that's what the police told her," I informed him, feeling a little guilty that I had spilled the beans about the murder.

Gary considered this for a moment. He had what looked like a fake tan and muscles peeked out from beneath the sleeves of his t-shirt. He looked younger than Carlisle, Skip, or Margie. Some people just age better than others.

"That's a terrible shame," he said after a moment. "Did they say what happened to him?"

"She said he had blunt force trauma to his head. I kind of wondered how the police knew he hadn't hit his head when he went into the water, but the detective said they were pretty sure that wasn't what happened."

"You asked the detective about it?" he asked. "Or did the police release this information to the public?"

I stopped for a second. I was saying too much. "That's just what I heard." I hoped I hadn't said too much, but I felt like I had.

"Well, that makes me feel even worse about Carlisle dying. I'd hate to think he might have suffered," he said sadly.

"Me too. I just can't imagine who might have done it. Everyone liked Carlisle," I said, glancing at the girls as they tried to pet each dog. They had moved on to the next kennel. "Oh, is it okay that they pet all the dogs?"

"We only put dogs that have passed the gentle test in these kennels," he said. "It's always good to keep an eye on them though."

"Girls, why don't you come back and pet the puppies?" I called. "They miss you."

The girls squealed and came back to the first two kennels that held at least three different litters of puppies of varying ages.

"I'll tell you something," Gary said and took a few steps away from the girls. I followed after him.

"What?" I asked.

"I do know one person that didn't like Carlisle much," he said, glancing over his shoulder.

"Who?"

"Mark Price. He lives in a trailer on Carlisle and Margie's property. He has a thing for Margie. Carlisle said he was worried about him being there," Gary whispered.

"Really?" I asked. "Carlisle was worried about him being there?"

He nodded. "Carlisle was really worried. He said Mark barged in on them one night when he was drunk and told Carlisle he and Margie were going to go away together. He said Margie told him that Mark was just crazy and she wouldn't leave him, but things weren't the same after that. Mark would glare at him and sometimes wouldn't speak to him at all when he came home from work."

"That's awful. Maybe you should talk to the detective about this," I suggested. "It might be good for him to know about it."

"I don't think so. I don't want to get involved," he said, shaking his head. "I'm sure the detective will look into that kind of thing, anyway. I bet he's talked to Mark already."

I nodded. "I'm sure he has. But you should at least think about talking to him."

"I'll think about it," he said, but he sounded like he already had his mind made up.

I wasn't sure what to make of all this. If what Gary said was true, it made me wonder if Mark was trying to get back at Margie by saying he thought she had killed Carlisle.

Chapter Eight

THE DAY OF CARLISLE'S funeral dawned clear and warm. The sky was a bright blue and a smattering of puffy clouds scudded across the sky. It was a beautiful day, and that made the funeral seem even more depressing. No one should be buried on a beautiful day.

The Baptist church was filling up fast when my mother, Stormy, and I slipped into a seat in the back. I was glad to see so many people had come to pay their last respects to Carlisle. It would make Margie feel good to see how many people cared about him.

"There are so many people here," Mom whispered.

"It's great, isn't it?" I said. "I think it will make Margie feel a little better knowing people care."

She nodded. "You can tell how many people you've touched in life by how many people show up to your funeral."

Margie was sitting in the front pew with an older, gray-haired woman that must have been Carlisle's mother. She dabbed at her eyes with a tissue now and then and it made my heart melt.

After a moment, Margie stood up. She was wearing a black dress and looked uncomfortable. Being a construction worker, I was pretty sure she wasn't accustomed to wearing dresses. She went to the casket, her ankles wobbling in her black low-heeled shoes and ran her hand over the dark wood.

"Good thing that casket is closed," Mom whispered. "I heard he had a head injury. No one needs to see that."

"Mom," I whispered. "Stop."

"What?" she asked. "I'm just stating the obvious."

"We don't need to hear the obvious," Stormy said. "We know what happened."

Mom sighed. "We need to keep an eye out for anyone acting guilty. The killer might be here."

"They might be," I agreed, and scanned the crowd. People were squeezing into the pews and were beginning to look like sardines. It was hard to get a good look at anyone when there were so many people squeezed into so small of a space.

"What does looking guilty look like?" Stormy asked, looking around the room.

"I don't know," I said. "But I bet we'll recognize it when we see it."

John Dewberry got up and went to Margie, and leaned in close to her, whispering something. John was a mailman and a nice guy. After a moment, Margie dabbed at her eyes with a tissue and then leaned over the casket, sobbing.

"Oh, no," I whispered. "Should we go help her?"

"Help her what?" Mom asked.

John took a small step back, patting her arm and looking awkward. He glanced out over the crowd, hoping for someone to step in.

"Mom, go talk to her," I hissed.

"You go talk to her. I'm not good with death," Mom hissed back.

I looked at Stormy and rolled my eyes. She shrugged. I wasn't going to get any help from Stormy either, so I got up and made my way down front. I could feel all eyes on me, and the minute John realized I was coming to rescue him, he nodded his appreciation and headed for his seat.

"Margie, I'm so sorry," I whispered and put a hand on her back.

Margie's sobs could be heard throughout the church. It broke my heart, and I wished someone else would come and offer their support along with me, but it looked like it was going to be all up to me.

"Margie, I wish I could say it was going to be okay, but I know this is so hard," I whispered. "I wish there was something I could say that would make you feel better, but I also know there isn't anything I can say."

After a moment, she straightened up and looked at me, her eyes red and swollen from her crying. "I don't know what I'll do without him. He was my whole world."

Her mascara ran down her cheeks, so I pulled a tissue out of a nearby box and dabbed at the streaks. "I'm sorry. This has got to be so hard."

She nodded. "Harder than I ever could have imagined. I'd just like to get this over with. Waiting to have a funeral feels like putting grieving on hold. This has been so hard on me and Carlisle's mama."

"It will be over soon," I said, patting her arm.

"That detective better find the killer. Or I'll find them. I am not going to sit idly by and let them go free," she suddenly said through gritted teeth.

"I'm sure he's doing all he can to find the killer," I assured her.

"I bet whoever killed him is here. Don't you think the killer is here?" she asked scanning the people in the pews.

"I don't know, Margie. We can't know that for sure," I pointed out.

She nodded. "Well, I'll figure it out and when I do, it will be the end of them."

I nodded. I didn't know what else to do. Margie needed to find a way to get through this funeral. I hoped she could control herself until after the funeral was over. She would regret it later if she didn't.

"Let me help you to your seat," I said and took her arm.

Once Margie was seated next to Carlisle's mother again, I headed back to my seat. I let my eyes run over the crowd as I went. Carlisle's killer had to be here. I suddenly had a feeling that went down to the bottom of my stomach. He or she was here. And where would you hide at a funeral if you were guilty? In the back, out of sight of most people, of course.

There was a wooden bench that ran along the back of the sanctuary. It was filled with familiar faces, all of whom looked innocent. Until my eyes landed on Mark Price. He was dressed in a navy blue polo shirt and black jeans. It was probably the closest thing he had to a nice suit. He sat right in the middle of the pew, with a gray-haired lady on either side of him.

I narrowed my eyes at him. Could he have done it? Living on Carlisle's property would certainly have given him opportunity. He would have known where Carlisle was most of the time. Carlisle would have trusted him. How easy would it have been for Mark to lure him to his death at the river? And if he had a thing for Carlisle's wife, that gave him motive.

I stopped at the end of the pew my mother and sister were sitting on, still looking at Mark. His eyes met mine, wide open and questioning. Were these the eyes of a killer? It made me wonder. I gave him a quick smile so he wouldn't know what I was thinking and then excused myself as I scooted past the three people at the end of the pew to sit next to Stormy.

Mark Price was someone that bore watching. If Cade Starkey weren't so pompous, I would have discussed it with him. As it was, I thought I would keep my suspicions to myself. For now, at least.

Chapter Nine

"SO, HOW DO YOU THINK the summer is going to shape up for you?" I asked Stormy. We had just been seated at our favorite Mexican restaurant and were looking over the menu. I knew that I wanted chicken enchiladas, but I always looked over the menu just in case. I didn't want to miss anything.

She sighed. "You know Natalie is leaving in August. I know exactly how the summer is going to shape up. Miserably."

"Stormy, don't think of it that way. Be excited. You did your job, and you did it well. Natalie is going to go to college, get an education, and then start a new career. It's one of the most exciting times of a young person's life," I assured her and took a sip of my iced tea.

"I know, I know. I guess I'm just being silly, aren't I?" she said, giving me a half-hearted smile. "I just can't believe how the last eighteen years just flew by. Weren't we just having her birthday parties at Chuck E. Cheese?"

"Sure seems that way," I agreed. Natalie had been so cute with her little blond braids and sky blue eyes. "And just think. It probably won't be too long before she meets the man of her dreams and gives you and Bob some cute little blond grandbabies."

Her eyes got big, and she went pale. "Don't you say that! Do you hate me? Why would you say that?"

I laughed. "Stop it, Stormy. That's supposed to be one of the most exciting things in the whole world. All the fun of having little ones and none of the financial responsibility. It's similar to having nieces and nephews. I enjoy it immensely."

"So, tell me, Rainey. When are you going to have a baby? You don't have much time, you know," she said, slickly changing the subject.

"Apparently, when pigs fly," I said, closing my menu and setting it on the edge of the table. "It doesn't seem to be in the cards anytime soon."

"You better get on it. You'll miss more than you can imagine if you don't," she said. "I think I'm going with the chimichangas."

"I'll miss what? Dirty diapers, getting up in the middle of the night, and toddlers getting every cold and flu that crosses their paths?" I asked lightly.

But she was right. If I was going to do it, I needed to get working on it. The problem was I didn't have anyone to make babies with. Maybe a puppy would be a good substitute for having a baby.

"You don't want to miss it," she said again and took a sip of her iced tea. "How's the cookbook coming?"

"Not bad. I've decided on an Americana theme. I've got several dessert recipes that I think I'll use. I still need to work on almost everything else though."

"How is your arrangement going with Sam?" she asked, sitting back in her seat.

"Not bad. He's been pretty happy with what I've been making for the diner. I think I'm going to try to come up with some barbecue recipes. They'll fit in just right at the diner," I said. "And, I have tentatively come up with a list of literary agents that I'm going to contact with a synopsis in the next month or so."

With Sam allowing me to try out new recipes at the diner, what I really wanted was to get the customer's opinions on the dishes. I was developing a lot of new recipes and enjoying getting to cook again. For the first time since the divorce, I felt like things were headed in the right direction for me.

"That's awesome about the agent! I'm happy for you, Rainey. I know how much you love cooking," she said. "And if you ever feel the need to get more opinions, remember that you can come to my house and make dinner for us anytime you want."

"Thanks. I do love all the cooking," I said. "I may take you up on making dinner for your family. That way I can gauge how kid-friendly some of the recipes are."

The waitress arrived, took our orders and brought out chips and salsa for the table. The best part about Mexican restaurants is the chips and salsa. I was pretty sure I could eat my weight in chips if allowed to.

"Rainey, look over there," she whispered, nodding to her left.

I looked and saw Margie Garlock and Mark Price at a table, digging into their own bowls of chips and salsa.

I turned back to Stormy. "I didn't expect to see her here." The funeral had been the day before and I suppose I had thought we wouldn't see Margie around town for a few days. It seemed like it had been an exhausting experience for her.

"I told you. They're seeing each other," she whispered.

"You don't know that," I said, turning to look again. They were deep in conversation and hadn't noticed us yet.

"What else do you think they're doing? Consoling each other with chips and salsa?"

"You're so funny," I said without looking at her. "Maybe she just needed to get away from it all. Margie had a hard time at the funeral yesterday. Mark's probably just keeping her company." I still didn't trust him, but if he had killed Carlisle, I didn't know how to prove it.

"Get away from what?" she asked. "I think there's something up with them."

"Maybe. But my money is on Mark."

I was still struggling to believe Margie could have killed Carlisle. Even though she had the physical brawn to do it, I still couldn't wrap my head around her having the heart to do it.

"I don't feel right about him, either," she whispered.

"Maybe Mark tried to break up a fight between them and accidentally killed Carlisle. Maybe Margie feels guilty about it and is keeping it quiet."

She turned to look at me. "I bet that's it. They had some kind of fight. I bet it was an accident. I don't think Margie would do it on purpose, either."

I nodded. "I think that's a real possibility. And maybe Mark told me he thought it was Margie so that if the police figured out it was the two of them, he had a story all made up so she'd take the fall."

"Are you going to tell the detective?" she asked.

"No, I am not going to tell him a thing," I said and dipped a chip into the salsa.

"Why not? He needs to know," she said and followed my lead.

"Mmm, these are the best chips in town," I said, crunching down on the chip. It was light and airy with just the right amount of salt. "Because the detective is a jerk. That's why."

She narrowed her eyes at me. "He'd make pretty babies. You should try being nicer to him. Play your cards right, and you could be in baby heaven."

I gasped. "Don't you say that! I detest that man."

"Such strong feelings," she teased. "Sounds to me like there's something going on there."

"Don't you start," I warned. "He's a jerk."

She sat there grinning at me and I decided to ignore her and enjoy my chips and salsa.

Chapter Ten

"HOW WAS THE MAC AND cheese?" I asked Sam.

Stormy and I had stopped by the diner after lunch to check on my latest recipe. I had put it together and put it into the oven after the breakfast shift so it would be available for the lunch rush. At my request, Sam bought a cute chalkboard to set near the hostess station. Changing the day's special on a chalkboard was a lot easier than changing the menu on a regular basis. It also allowed me to make something on a whim and just add it to the board.

"It was really awesome and the customers loved it. Nice and cheesy," he said, wiping down the kitchen counter. The diner had just closed and he and the waitresses were cleaning up so they could go home. "Hi Stormy."

"Hi Sam," she said.

"Hey Ron," I said to our dishwasher. "Did you get a chance to try out the mac and cheese?"

Ron Walker was in his early sixties and was a slight guy, no more than five-feet-four-inches tall, with a faded tattoo of an anchor and hula girl on his bicep. He glanced over his shoulder at me. "Yeah, Rainey, it was great. I could have eaten my weight in that mac and cheese. You're a really good cook."

The praise made me smile. I would never get tired of hearing that someone had enjoyed the food I made. "Thanks, guys. I'm glad you liked it."

"I loved it, too," Luanne said, pulling off her apron and tossing it into the dirty linens hamper. "You should make more items to add to the menu."

"Thanks, Luanne. I appreciate hearing that. I'll make as much as I can."

Luanne stopped and looked at Stormy. "You know, you two look so much alike, it's scary."

Stormy shot me a look.

"That's because we're identical twins," Stormy said to her.

Luanne nodded. "Yeah, I know." She turned and left the kitchen, leaving Stormy looking after her.

Stormy turned and looked at me again and I shook my head.

"That detective was in here looking for you, Rainey," Sam said. He brushed back his brown hair with his fingers. It was getting too long, and he needed a haircut.

"Me? Why would he be looking for me?" I asked, leaning against the kitchen counter.

He shrugged. "He didn't say. He just came in for lunch and asked about you. He seems to come in here a lot lately, don't you think?" There was a twinkle in his eye when he said it and it irritated me.

"I haven't noticed," I lied. The truth was, I had noticed. Of course, he had been doing an investigation over the past few weeks after Celia Markson died in our parking lot, and now that

Carlisle had died, he was looking into his death. We were seeing a lot of him and I was glad Carlisle hadn't died here at the diner. I didn't like answering questions about a murder.

I looked at Stormy and she mimicked rocking a baby in her arms. I glared at her.

"Well, he has been here a lot," Sam said again, scrubbing the grill.

Ron turned back and looked at me. "That was terrible what happened to Carlisle. You know, I heard from my friend Rick Frost that Gary Dunning as at the bar, telling people Carlisle had it coming. I thought that was strange since they were such good friends."

"What? I spoke to Gary yesterday, and he seemed genuinely saddened by his death," I said.

Sam turned to look at Ron. "That doesn't make sense. Why would Gary say that publicly?"

He shrugged. "He was in a bar. Maybe he'd had too much to drink and his real feelings came out. Or maybe he was just brooding over something that had happened a long time ago and with a little alcohol, he got stirred up over it."

"I don't know. He seemed genuinely sad when I talked to him. This is a small town and you know how things get said and then passed around," I said. "I could be wrong, but I don't think he would say that. Did Rick hear it himself? Or did he hear it from someone else?"

Ron shrugged again. "I don't know. I'm only passing on what I heard from him."

"That's the problem with rumors," Sam said, turning back to the grill. "They get passed around and no one really knows where it started and it changes a little with each telling. Kind of like the old game of telephone."

"That's the truth," I agreed.

"Okay, I guess you're right. But Rick sure seemed to know what he was talking about," Ron said and turned back to the sink to finish washing the dishes.

And that really was the way of rumors. I sighed. One thing was for sure. I was not going to tell Detective Cade Starkey about anything I'd heard. He'd only lecture me on not getting involved.

"Rainey, can you make some linguine for the menu?" Luanne asked, bringing a tray full of dirty dishes into the kitchen for Ron to wash.

"Um, no, linguine is an Italian dish and I'm focusing on American dishes for my cookbook," I explained.

She set the tray down on the counter top and turned toward me. "But, America is a melting pot of countries, therefore, an Italian dish fits in with the theme of your cookbook."

I narrowed my eyes at her. "Yes, but I want to use recipes that originated here in the Untied States."

"Lots of Italians originate here in America. Haven't you heard of Italian Americans?" she asked, unloading the tray and setting the dirty dishes next to the sink for Ron to wash.

Sam grinned at me from his place by the grill and I gave him a look.

"Luanne, I want to use recipes that American housewives have used in this country since the last century," I explained.

She nodded. "Good. Please make the linguine. Make it Italian American so it will fit in your cookbook."

I sighed. "Sure. I'll see what I can come up with."

It was easier to agree with her than to try and explain it again. I hated to admit it, but she did have some logic in her what she said. Sort of. I might make her some linguine, but I was not going to include it in the cookbook.

"I guess we'll get going. See you all tomorrow," I said and Stormy and I headed out to my car.

What Ron said made me wonder again about Gary. Was he pretending to be upset about Carlisle's death when I spoke to him? At this point, anything was possible.

Chapter Eleven

"DO YOU THINK YOU'RE going to get some work done around here today?" Georgia asked, putting one hand on her hip. Her dyed and streaked auburn hair was cut in a bob and she would have been cute if it weren't for the snarl on her lips.

I sighed. Georgia complained about everyone, but it felt like I had a special place in her heart. She never let up.

"I'll be right there," I said. I set the tray of chocolate donuts I had just pulled out of the oven onto the kitchen counter. I had gotten to the diner early and whipped up a batch of the tasty morsels, but I wasn't feeling confident. There was something not quite right about them and I hated when a recipe didn't go as planned. "Maybe I shouldn't sell these to the customers."

"They'll be fine," Sam assured me from the grill. "And don't pay any attention to Georgia. You know how she is."

"I know exactly how she is," I muttered, looking the donuts over. The scent of chocolate filled the kitchen, and I inhaled. "Do you really think they're okay?"

"I've already eaten two from the first batch. Believe me, they're really great," he said and flipped a pancake.

The smell of pancakes made me sad about Carlisle again. I wasn't sure I would ever be able to smell them again without thinking about him.

"Okay, I'll take your word for it," I said and began moving the cooled donuts from the first batch to a serving plate. I hoped Sam wasn't just trying to make me feel better. Some days I had doubts about the food I made. I wasn't sure I would ever get over it. I liked to think it kept me humble. On other days, I thought I must be the most gifted cook and baker in the world. Yeah, I needed the humbling at times.

"They're great," he repeated.

I brought the plate of donuts out to the front counter and set them out where they could be seen, placing a glass cover over them.

That will work, I thought.

I looked up when the diner door swung open. Margie stood in the doorway and the look on her face told me she wasn't a happy camper.

When she spotted me behind the front counter, she narrowed her eyes at me.

"Rainey!" she nearly shouted.

"Margie?" I asked.

She strode over to the counter and stood in front of me. "You have some nerve! How can you live with yourself?" Her face was red as she stood to her entire nearly six-feet-tall height.

"What are you talking about Margie? What's going on?" I asked. Margie was an imposing woman and when she was angry, she was even more so. I wondered how often Carlisle had faced her when she was this angry and I also wondered what had made her this angry.

She took a deep breath and for a moment I saw tears in her eyes. She blinked them back. "I know what you and Stormy did yesterday, and so do you!"

I swallowed. *What had we done?*

"Margie, I'm not sure what you're talking about," I said trying to sound calm. I wasn't sure what she was upset about.

"My neighbor was in the La Casa restaurant when the two of you decided to talk about me. Do you know how much that hurts? I've always thought kindly of you and your sister," she said as tears sprang to her eyes again.

I gasped. "I'm so sorry Margie," I said, as my heart pounded in my chest. What had we done? "We didn't mean anything by it. We just want Carlisle's killer found."

"By suspecting me?" she asked.

People in the diner were beginning to stare. "Margie, I do not think you killed Carlisle," I whispered. "I don't know who did, but both Stormy and I want that person found more than anything in the world. I'm sorry. Maybe your neighbor misunderstood what was said."

My mind scrambled to remember what we talked about. Both Stormy and I thought that if Mark Price had killed Carlisle, it was probably an accident and that Margie had nothing to do with it. I felt terrible for having talked about her where someone could overhear us.

She shook her head. "Rainey, you have no idea how hard this has been."

"I'm so sorry," I said. "We didn't mean any harm. Stormy and I said we didn't think you could have hurt Carlisle. But, we shouldn't have been discussing it where someone could overhear. Please forgive us."

Margie stared at me a moment, her face lightening up to pink instead of its former red, and then she shook her head. "I'm probably blowing things out of proportion. Everyone in town is talking about Carlisle's murder. I'm sorry, I shouldn't have yelled at you."

"No, it's me and Stormy that should have kept our mouths shut. Listen, Margie, we really just want the police to find Carlisle's killer. Is there anything you can think of that will help the police track down the killer?"

She shook her head. "I've been over and over things in my mind. I don't know. I asked Mark if he had any idea or if Carlisle mentioned someone that he might have had trouble with, but he had no idea."

I nodded. "Margie, are you and Mark close?" I asked, lowering my voice. I was thinking about the rumors that said the two of them were an item. I didn't expect her to tell me they were having an affair, but I did wonder what she would say about him.

"I've worked with him for over five years. His ex-wife was a friend. Why do you ask?"

I shrugged. "Would you like a donut, Margie? On the house?" I said and got a plate, putting two donuts on it. "I just wondered is all."

She sat down on Carlisle's stool. "He's been good to rent to. We needed the rent money he gives us for living in the trailer.

He really came at a good time. Carlisle and I had a lot of repairs we needed to make on the house and the money was a real boost to our finances."

I nodded, setting the plate in front of her and giving her a fork. The chocolate frosting was a little messy but was delicious. Then I got her a cup of coffee and put that down in front of her.

"Do you think he's a good person? Someone you can trust?" I asked her.

"Sure," she said slowly. "What are you getting at?"

"Nothing, Margie. I just wondered."

"That detective keeps asking me questions. I feel like he thinks I'm responsible," she whispered. Her eyes went wide as she looked at me. "I would never do that. Even if I didn't love him I couldn't kill him. But I do love him, so there's no way I could do that."

"Margie, can I be honest with you?" I asked her. I was probably going out on a ledge here, but she needed to know the truth.

"Yes, sure," she said, picking up the fork. "These look good."

"Mark may have mentioned that he thought you might have something to do with Carlisle's death," I said as gently as I could. "I mean, he didn't come out and say it. Not exactly anyway."

Margie gasped, staring at me with fork poised over the donuts. "What did he say?"

I swallowed. Was I getting in too deep? Probably so, but I had to know the truth. "He thought the two of you fought a lot. He thought maybe an argument had gotten out of hand and maybe it was an accident."

She stared at me. "That is not true. Sure, we argued. Don't all couples? But that doesn't mean anything. I can't believe he would say that!"

"Maybe we can sort this out," I said thoughtfully. "Where were you the night Carlisle died? Mark said you weren't home." I didn't know if Margie was keeping something to herself or not, but it felt like she was. Maybe there was something she didn't want known.

"Do you think Mark went to the detective and told him I killed Carlisle?" her voice cracked when she asked it.

"I don't really know," I said. "Were you gone that night?"

She looked at me and then looked away. "It was the night before they found him. I went shopping over in Boise. I wasn't supposed to be spending money. We were trying really hard to pay off some bills with the rent money Mark paid us. Even with the rent money, we had gone into debt to repair the house. We wanted it all done at once, and didn't want to wait to have the money in hand, so we took out a loan. Carlisle was determined not to stay in debt, but we had been on such a tight budget for so long, that I got tired of it and just went shopping."

"Well, that's understandable," I said. "Sometimes you just need to buy yourself a little something. Did you tell the detective this?"

Her face went pink again. "No." She cut into one of the donuts with her fork and took a bite. "Wow, Rainey, this is good. Really good. So moist."

"Thanks. Why didn't you tell the detective? You were just out shopping, so what would it matter?" It didn't make sense to me that she wouldn't tell him.

"Because. I didn't just buy a little something. I blew the whole month's rent payment and put a couple hundred dollars on a credit card. I don't know why I did it. Before we got married, I had a spending problem. I guess even after we were married, I still had a problem, and I got us into debt. I'm not proud of it."

"Okay, so you spent a lot of money. I'm still not seeing why you wouldn't tell the detective."

She sighed. "When I got home, Carlisle and I had a fight about the money I spent. It went on for a long while and ended with Carlisle slamming the door and leaving. When he didn't come home that night, I thought he was just mad. I figured he went to spend the night at his mother's. He did things like that sometimes. He would get mad at me and then go cry on his mother's shoulder. It made things tense between us sometimes."

"That's completely understandable that that might cause issues between the two of you," I said.

"I should have looked for him. I should have called his mother at the very least, but I didn't," she said and began crying.

"I'm sorry Margie," I said. It was obvious she was consumed with guilt and my heart went out to her. "When did you begin to worry about him?"

"When I hadn't heard from him by the following evening. I searched everywhere for him, but I couldn't find him," she said and wiped her eyes with a napkin. "I finally called the police late that evening."

"Margie, you can't even report a missing person for 24 hours. It's not like you did anything wrong," I said trying to make her feel better.

"But I could have tried to find him," she insisted. "If I would have called someone, I might have been able to keep him from going wherever it was that the murderer was."

"Didn't anyone at his job miss him?" I asked.

"Yes, they tried to call me, but I had left my phone at home so I didn't have to answer it if he called. It was childish. I was mad at him and I didn't want to speak to him. Right now, I'd give anything to talk to him one last time," she said as tears sprang to her eyes.

I nodded. "I'm so sorry Margie," I said. "But you can't blame yourself for what happened."

She looked into my eyes. "I will always blame myself for Carlisle's death."

She was right. If I had been in her position, I would feel the same way. It was a terrible situation to be in. I patted her hand. "Let me know if I can do anything for you."

She nodded. "Thank you, Rainey. But you know something? Since Mark's throwing me under the bus, I guess I may as well say it. Earlier that day, Mark argued with Carlisle. I don't know what it was about, but I heard them out near the trailer. When Carlisle came into the house he was steaming mad. That's why we fought so badly. He was already upset. Poor thing. I bet he felt like he was getting hit from all sides."

I bet he did feel that way, I thought. Poor Carlisle. He had taken his troubles to his grave.

Chapter Twelve

I STEWED OVER THE CONVERSATION I had had with Margie the rest of the day. Mark was definitely manipulative. How could he tell me, and maybe Cade, that Margie had had arguments with Carlisle and that she was probably the killer? It was convenient that he left out the fact he had also argued with Carlisle. I also felt terrible about Stormy and I talking about Margie and being overheard.

After work, I did what I knew I shouldn't. I went looking for Mark. I had no business doing it, but the more I thought about it, the more I felt I had to.

I drove over to the construction site and parked. I didn't see Margie's car, and I wondered if she had taken the day off. I may have made working conditions tense between the two of them by telling Margie what Mark had told me, but it had to be said.

I got out of my car and went to look for Mark. There were several other construction workers looking over some plans and I passed by them, peering into the houses that had no solid walls yet. I found him inside the house at the far end of the site.

He looked up when I approached. "Hi, uh, Rainey?" he said with a hesitant smile.

"Hello, Mark," I said. I didn't want to be friendly with him, so I didn't smile back. "I have a question for you, Mark. Why did you lie to me about Margie?"

His face fell. "What do you mean?"

"You know what I mean. You told me you thought she killed Carlisle. You lied to me and you probably told the detective the same thing. You know she didn't kill him." I put my hands in my jeans pockets for something to do with them. But I wanted to do more than that. I was itching to try out some kickboxing moves on him.

"Now, wait a minute. You asked me about what happened and I told you. They argued a lot. It wouldn't surprise me at all if she killed him. She's so much bigger than he was, and she has a temper," he said. "How is that a lie?"

I snorted. "Don't play innocent with me. I never asked you about either Margie or Carlisle. You approached me at the gas station and you led me to believe something by twisting the facts. The truth is, you had your own arguments with Carlisle. If you were going to tell me that Margie argued with him, why didn't you tell me that you argued with him as well?"

"Listen," he said straightening up and coming toward me. "Why are you even asking about this? It's none of your business."

"No, it isn't my business. But you volunteered the information. Were you hoping I would tell the detective so you wouldn't have to? You call yourself her friend, but you manipulated the facts," I said, putting my hands on my hips.

He shook his head, and stepped closer to me. I involuntarily took a step back. There were witnesses, so I didn't think he would try to do anything to me, but if he did, I felt pretty confident I could handle him.

"Listen, Rainey. You are Rainey, aren't you?" he asked, lowering his voice.

I nodded.

"Rainey, here's the thing. I do appreciate that Carlisle and Margie let me live on their property. But Margie, she got funny after a while. She kept saying things like how much she enjoyed having me around. It didn't take long before I realized that she had feelings for me. Feelings I had no intention of returning," he said, and glanced over his shoulder. "I didn't want to hurt her."

"Maybe you were reading more into things than was actually there?" I suggested.

"No. I swear I wasn't. I didn't want to get in the middle of those two. They're nice people."

"Did you tell her you weren't interested? It seems like that would have been the easiest thing to do," I said.

"No, that's not an easy thing to do. I needed to live in the trailer for a while longer. I thought if I let Margie know I wasn't interested in her, she might get mad and make me move. I was homeless for a while and I don't ever want to go back to that."

I rolled my eyes. "It seems like doing the right thing should have been a no-brainer. You just tell her you respect both of them too much to jeopardize your relationship. She would have respected you for that."

"I did what I felt I had to do," he said, raising his chin in defiance.

"You still haven't told me why you said you thought she might have killed Carlisle," I pointed out.

He shrugged. "I guess I was overthinking everything. Carlisle was my friend and I was worried about who might have killed him. I should have kept my mouth shut."

I rolled my eyes. "I think you're just full of excuses."

"I'm telling you the truth!" he insisted.

"Are you, Mark? Because I don't think you are," I said, narrowing my eyes at him.

He shook his head and looked away, and then back at me. "Listen. I need to get back to work," he said. "I didn't mean to hurt Margie and I didn't kill Carlisle."

"Did you tell the detective that you suspected Margie?" I asked.

"What? No! I didn't say anything to him. I gotta get back to work now." With that he turned and went back to the house he had been working on.

I watched him go, wondering if he was telling the truth. He had had no issues approaching me at the gas station and telling me what he thought had happened to Carlisle. Why wouldn't he tell the detective the same thing?

"I'D LIKE TO SPEAK TO Detective Starkey," I told the woman at the front desk at the police station.

She sighed loudly. Clearly, I was disturbing her.

"Hold on," she said and picked up the phone. "Yeah, you got someone out here that wants to talk to you. Fine." She hung up the phone without saying goodbye. "Go through that door, and all the way to the end of the hall. His office is on the left."

"Thanks," I said and headed to the door. The station smelled a little musty. The afternoon sun was hot and I considered suggesting she open a window, but decided against it.

When I got to the last door on the left, I raised my hand to knock, but the door opened before my knuckles made contact with it.

"Rainey?" Cade said, with his eyebrows raised.

I nodded. "Can I talk to you a minute?"

I was probably making a mistake, coming to speak to him, but here I was. I had nothing to lose now.

"Sure, come on in," he said and led me to a chair in front of his desk.

His office was sparsely furnished, with a desk, two visitors' chairs and the desk chair. There was a small table in the corner that held a printer and a small coffee pot.

"This is nice," I said and sat down. I may have lied a little.

He went behind his desk and sat down. "Yeah, I think the same thing every time I come to work. What's up?" he asked with a smirk.

I put my hands in my lap. "I know it isn't my business, but can I ask what's going on with Carlisle Garlock's murder investigation?"

"You're right, it isn't your business. Why are you asking about it?" he asked. "If I remember right, I told you to mind your own business."

I sighed. "Look, I think someone may be saying things that aren't true and I wanted to make sure you know the truth," I explained.

"What would that truth be?" he asked, leaning back in his chair.

"Mark Price told me he thought Margie killed Carlisle. He's lying. She didn't do it," I said, and leaned back in my own chair.

"And how do you know Margie is telling you the truth?"

My mouth opened, then I closed it. He had a point, but I wasn't going to admit it. "Because it's a feeling I have. I know her well enough to say she didn't do it."

"So, you want me to conduct my investigation based on your feelings?" he asked, raising those darned eyebrows again.

"Well, not exactly. But you're new to town. You don't know people around here like I do," I pointed out.

He looked at me for longer than was comfortable before speaking again. "Actually, gut feelings can be important in an investigation. We can't go by that alone, obviously, because people surprise us all the time. And you're right. You do know people around here that I don't know. But, it's still early in the investigation. Everyone is a suspect."

"Did Mark tell you he thought Margie was the killer because she and Carlisle fought all the time?" I asked.

"He did tell me that," he admitted.

I gasped. "See that? He just told me not even twenty minutes ago that he didn't tell you that! He's a liar and if he will lie about one thing, he'll lie about another."

He grinned. "Rainey, why are you getting involved in this? It seems odd that you're sticking your nose in it, especially after I told you not to."

"Because Margie is a friend and I don't want to see her railroaded. Innocent people go to jail all the time."

"No one is railroading anyone. We want to find the killer much more than you do, believe me. I can appreciate that you feel like you need to help find the killer because Margie's your friend, but it's none of your business. If you have any actual evidence, of course I want to see it. But I can't go on your gut feeling," he said, leaning forward. "Tell me you won't get any further involved in this."

I looked at him. "I won't get further involved."

"You're lying, right?"

I stuck my chin out. It made me angry that he thought he could tell me what to do. "I might be. Or maybe not. You never can tell."

"Well, according to some people, if someone will lie about one thing, they'll lie about another."

I had to force myself not to smile. I wasn't going to be friendly with him no matter what he said. "Fine."

"Rainey. Please don't get involved. I don't want you to get hurt. You just might make the killer angry," he said softly.

I took a deep breath. "Okay. I just wanted you to know about Mark Price."

"Duly noted," he said.

I nodded and got to my feet. "I'll see you around."

I left the police station. Was I making a mistake talking to him? I didn't know, but I didn't like the fact that Mark had lied and was obviously manipulating both Cade and me.

Chapter Thirteen

WHEN I GOT HOME, THERE was a dogcatcher's truck parked in front of the house. I pulled into the driveway and got out of my car.

"Hi, Gary," I said as he got out of his truck.

"Hi, Rainey," he said, closing the door. "I got a call that there was a stray dog in this neighborhood. German shepherd. Have you seen it?"

"I just got off work," I said, glancing around. "I didn't see one before I left this morning. I hope it's friendly."

"Hopefully," he said. "We don't want him to bite anyone and I'm sure his family is worried about him."

"Poor thing. He's probably scared," I said.

"We'll get him found," he assured me.

"So, how are things going at work?" I asked. It had only been a few days since I had seen him at the shelter, but I wondered how he and his coworkers were handling things.

"As well as can be expected. The funeral was hard to get through," he said. "You just never think about attending your friend's funeral until you have to do it."

"I agree. It doesn't seem real," I said. "I can't imagine what poor Margie's going through."

"Are the police any closer to getting the murder solved?" he asked. "I hate the thought that there's a killer on the loose. I know Margie will sleep better once they find whoever it was."

"I really don't think the police have any idea who did it yet," I said. "I guess the river may have washed away any clues."

He nodded. "To be honest, it wouldn't surprise me if they figure out he just slipped into the river. There was a storm the night before and I'm sure the banks of the river were slippery. With him not being able to swim, it would have been easy to just slip into the water and be washed away with the current."

"That's true. But why would he have been out there at that hour?" I asked, leaning against his truck.

"Didn't you know? He got a call to go out there late the night before. Someone called in a dog that looked starved that had been hanging around the riverbank. It wouldn't come to whoever called it in, so they called us."

"Really?" I asked. "I hadn't heard that."

Was he telling the truth? Margie had said he'd been home and stormed off after their fight. I supposed there could have been an emergency call that he answered that Margie wasn't aware of. And then Ron had mentioned his friend overhearing Gary saying Carlisle had it coming. It gave me something to think about.

He nodded. His blond hair was short, but it looked as if he hadn't combed it that morning. There was a tuft on the side of his head that stuck straight out to the side.

"I'm not exactly sure, but I think it's a pretty good bet that he was out there right as that storm got started. Honestly, I don't know why the police are spending so much time looking at this like it's a murder. Carlisle was a good guy and people liked him. I can't think of one person that would have wanted him dead."

"I have to agree with that. I can't think of anyone that would want to dead him, either," I said. And it was true. I was as puzzled by his death as anyone else.

"But, you know what they say. You never know what goes on behind closed doors. Maybe Margie got tired of him and offed him." He said the last part with a grin.

"That's kind of rude, don't you think?" I asked. I was taken aback by his remark.

He shrugged. "Sorry. That was a little misplaced levity."

I remembered what Agatha had said about Gary being bitter about not getting the position at the shelter. Was it true?

"How was Carlisle to work for, Gary? With him being the director, that made him your boss, didn't it?" I asked, tilting my head and watching him closely.

The grin left his face. "Oh, you know. Carlisle was Carlisle. He was easygoing." He shrugged. "I guess things could have been better. I think everyone thinks that about their job though."

"That's true. There's always room for improvement on any job. The community sure was glad to have him in charge though. Getting the county shelter to be a no-kill shelter was huge. People are always talking about what a wonderful accomplishment that was."

He looked off into the sky for a moment and then back at me. "Well, I guess I better get going. I've got a dog to catch," he said abruptly. "Give me a call if you see that dog, will you?"

"I sure will," I said. "Keep up the good work."

He nodded and got back into his truck and started it. I headed toward my front door. I wondered if Gary was as excited to work for Carlisle as he said he was. He was acting odd and I didn't like him throwing Margie's name back into the ring. She had to be innocent. At least, that was what I was hoping for.

I PULLED OUT A BAG of chocolate chips and unsweetened baking chocolate from the cupboard. How much more American could you get than brownies? I debated as to whether brownies would be special enough to put into the new cookbook or not. I sighed. Who cared if they were special enough? I had a craving for brownies.

I pulled out the rest of the ingredients and got to work, mixing the dry ingredients together. When I was a kid, it seemed my mother made brownies every weekend. My sister and I had cut our teeth on them.

As I worked on making the brownies, my mind went over what I knew about Carlisle's death. Was it still possible he had just had an unfortunate accident? Wasn't it possible Cade was wrong? I wondered how often that happened. Innocent people went to jail all the time and by that same token, I thought it was entirely possible that freak accidental deaths could be thought to be murder. If that were the case, how would the police realize the truth? I also wondered if Cade had gotten the final autopsy report. But Cade would never tell me if he had gotten it and if he had, he certainly wouldn't tell me what was on it.

I popped the pan of brownies into the oven and lay down on the sofa while they baked. My mother's longhaired ginger cat, Poofy, jumped on my chest, demanding attention and I turned the TV on.

I must have been more tired than I thought because before I knew it, I was asleep and dreaming. Standing on the banks of the Snake River, I saw something being washed down river. When I looked up into the sky, dark storm clouds were swirling and I could hear the distant rumble of thunder. I squinted my eyes as light raindrops fell on my face. My eyes went back to the river and the large mass in the river had floated closer. To my horror, I realized it was Carlisle. He had a head wound and blood trickled down his face.

I opened my mouth to call out to him when I realized his eyes were open. His mouth opened and closed as he tried to tell me something.

"Carlisle!" I called, stepping closer to the water.

He reached a hand out to me and I looked down at the muddy banks I was standing on to find a rope or a tree branch to throw to him. I spotted a life preserver just lying on the ground and as I reached for it, my feet slipped. I screamed and tried to scramble up on the bank and away from the flowing river. My hands couldn't make purchase on anything solid and my feet entered the water.

When I looked back over my shoulder, I saw Carlisle, still in the middle of the river. There was a sinister grin on his face that sent cold chills through my body and I screamed.

The timer for the brownies woke me with a start, and Poofy dug her claws into my chest as I jumped.

"Ow, Poofy, let go," I said, and set her on the floor. My heart was pounding in my chest. I wasn't sure if Carlisle was trying to tell me something from beyond the grave or if I had just been thinking about him too much.

The dream ran through my mind again and I shuddered and got to my feet. The house was filled with the scent of chocolate and I headed to the kitchen, shaking off the memory of the dream.

Poor Carlisle.

Chapter Fourteen

THE LULL BETWEEN BREAKFAST and lunch was my favorite time of the day at the diner. It gave me a chance to rest a couple of minutes before the lunch rush began. My feet were aching from running around bringing people coffee and ketchup for their hash browns. I heaved my aching body onto a stool at the front counter. Diane sat on the stool beside me.

"My poor feet," she said with a sigh.

"Mine, too," I agreed.

"Uh oh, here comes the boss," she kidded when Sam came out from the kitchen.

He smiled.

"The boss has aching feet, too." He leaned against the counter. "How's the cookbook coming, Rainey?"

"Not bad. I've been brainstorming and trying to come up with ideas. It's hard thinking up original ideas when the whole theme of the cookbook is Americana. I mean, they can't be completely original recipes because they've all already been done. So, I've been looking over old recipes from the last century."

I wanted something unique. Or at least, unique for the current century. I admired cooks from the past. It seemed like they relied on ingenuity far more than we did today. I could spend hours flipping through old cookbooks from the 1920s through 1950s. I never got bored. Cooking had changed a lot over the years and I felt like as a culture, we had lost some important recipes and cooking techniques and I wanted to bring them back.

"I can't wait to try out more of your recipes," Diane said. "Those donuts were great."

"Thanks. I'm still working on the recipe. I think it needs something else."

The door swung open and my mom walked through it. We all turned to look.

"Hi, Mrs. Daye," Sam said. "How are you this morning?"

She smiled. "I'm great. We got a big shipment of vases and gift items in at the flower shop, so I decided now was the time to take a walk and let my employees do the heavy lifting."

"That's nice of you, Mom," I said. "Reminds me of when Stormy and I were kids and cleaning day consisted of the two of us doing most of the work."

"It's fine. They love the work," she assured us. "You and Stormy loved it, too."

She took a seat at the counter. "I'm hungry for something sweet. My doctor wants me to eat more protein, but I like pie. Rainey, did you bring something new to try out today?"

"Not today. I didn't get up early enough," I said.

"Tsk, tsk," she said. "What have you got, Sam?"

"There are some cinnamon rolls left from breakfast," he said.

"I'll take one," Mom answered. "Cinnamon anything is my favorite."

"I'll get it," Diane said and jumped up.

"I saw Gary Dunning in the neighborhood after you left this morning, Rainey," Mom said.

"He was there yesterday, too," I said. "He was looking for a stray German shepherd."

"I haven't seen any stray dogs in the neighborhood," Mom said. "But I guess he's just doing his job."

"You gotta hand it to them. Those county guys do a good job," Sam said.

"Sam, did you know Gary was up for the promotion that Carlisle got? Those two were always rivals in high school," she said. "I guess some things never change."

"Really? All the way back to high school?" he asked.

She nodded as Diane set the cinnamon roll in front of her along with a cup of coffee. "If one got a place on one of the sports teams, the other had to try out. There were several times when the two of them got into fights at school over a girl. Gary had his eye on Margie, you know."

"Really?" I asked. This was news to me and I wondered why she hadn't mentioned it before.

"Yes, it seemed like Carlisle always got whatever Gary wanted. It makes you wonder how well he was handling having to work for Carlisle," she said.

Diane sat next to me again. "I heard he was pretty bitter about it," she said. "My cousin works at the shelter and she said he went to the board of directors and complained. She said he did have a point. Gary had nearly ten more years experience than Carlisle did, but Carlisle seemed to make friends a little easier. I'm sure that influenced the board to give the position to him."

"It makes you wonder," Mom said.

My mom was right. It did make me wonder. Could Gary have gotten fed up with coming behind Carlisle in everything and made sure it would never happen again?

Chapter Fifteen

WHEN I PULLED INTO the parking lot at the recreation area for the Snake River, it was only half-full. That surprised me. It was now early June, and the weather had turned nice after the storm we had had the night Carlisle died. I parked my car and got out.

It was a short hike to the riverbank and there were signs posted along the way warning people to stay out and stay alive. I walked all the way to the edge of the water and looked at the river as it ran its course.

Close to the bank, the water seemed innocuous. But as you waded further out into the water, it turned treacherous. Twenty years earlier one of my classmates had drowned out here, near the very spot where I stood. Hal Owens had been a loudmouth jock. He was on the football team and swore the world revolved around him. I had heard there was a party that summer night and when Hal went in for a swim, he didn't come back out until the sheriff's department pulled him from the river three miles away.

I shivered. My mother had taught us to be cautious. In high school, I had attended parties at the river, and fortunately everyone went home in one piece. But I never took risks here at the river.

I walked along the bank with my eyes on the ground. There wouldn't be anything to find at this late date that would tell the tale of how Carlisle died, but as I walked, I tried to imagine what had happened. Had Carlisle still been alive when he went in? Or had he already been dead? An image of Margie hitting him on the head with a monkey wrench sprang to mind, and I shook myself. Margie couldn't have done it. I was almost certain of that. The autopsy report would tell whether he was alive or dead when he went into the river. Whether Cade would tell me what that report said was anyone's guess.

I took a deep breath and walked around a family having a barbecue near the edge of the river. I smiled at the mom when I caught her eye and she smiled back.

There was a part of the riverbank that went up steeply as the water flowed down the edge of a small hill. The bank formed a low cliff, not more than a few feet high. I knelt beside the beginning of it. The soil had been washed away in this area. Was it simply the swift rushing water that had eroded the side of the cliff? Or had there been a struggle, with dirt being knocked into the river? I ran a hand over a spot that had broken away. There wouldn't be a way to tell now.

Carlisle wasn't a swimmer. He would have been extra cautious in this area. Why would he come near this place, anyway? If he had been hunting a stray dog, it seemed like the dog would have hung around the recreation area where it might find scraps of food left behind by people. I couldn't remember if

Cade or Margie had mentioned where Carlisle was pulled from the river. It could have been miles from here.

I looked up and saw Cade Starkey on the other side of the embankment. He looked at me with one eyebrow arched.

"Fancy meeting you here," he called above the rushing water.

I straightened up. "What a surprise," I said and backed away from the embankment.

He climbed up and over the area I had been looking at, and small amounts of the soil gave way as he did.

"What are you doing, Rainey?" he asked, fixing me with those green eyes of his.

"Nothing at all," I said, glancing away. "It was a nice day for a walk, so that's what I'm doing. Going for a walk."

He nodded with a smile. "There's nothing out here. We've been over and over this area, as well as the area where Carlisle was pulled from the water, four miles away."

"Four miles?" I asked.

He nodded. "That storm had the water flowing quickly that night."

"It still doesn't explain why he was out here," I said, stepping backward as he came closer.

"The shelter received a report of a stray dog in this area. That was why he came out here," he said. "What are you looking for?"

So it was true. There had been a report of a dog out here.

I took a step back and shook my head. "Nothing. I told you, I just went for a walk."

"Listen, Rainey. I don't know why you have an interest in this case, but it isn't your business. Can't you just leave things alone?" he asked.

His tone wasn't unkind, but I had been caught doing what he had told me not to do. I felt defensive.

"I told you. Carlisle and Margie are my friends. I'm interested in what happened to him."

"I get that. I really do. But you don't have any business sticking your nose into this. It isn't safe."

I nodded. "I swear I was just going for a walk. It's a nice day."

He looked up at the sky for a moment, then back at me. "Fine. Go for a walk. But stay out of trouble. Can you do that?"

I smiled. "Of course. I don't like trouble much, so I'll stay clear of it."

"That's what I want to hear," he said.

We stood and looked at each other for longer than was necessary or comfortable. Cade Starkey had a good poker face because I had no idea what he was thinking.

"I guess I'll get going now," I finally said and took another step back. I was suddenly feeling nervous.

He nodded. "Rainey," he said and then paused.

"Yes?" I asked.

He looked out at the river and then back at me. "Just, don't do anything stupid. I've never met anyone that seemed to want to get into trouble as much as you do."

I sighed. "I told you. I don't like trouble. I've got to get home, anyway. I've got some baking to do."

"Great. I hope you bring it to the diner. I'd like to try more of your baking. I have a bit of a sweet tooth, and the diner has become one of my favorite eating establishments."

"I'm sure I'll bring something to the diner. I've been working on a lot of new recipes. I'll see you around," I said and turned and headed back in the direction I had come from.

That detective was an odd person if you asked me. For a moment I thought he was going to ask me something important. And for a moment, it seemed like I wanted him to. I pushed back the thought. I had no need of him or anyone else in my life.

Chapter Sixteen

I GLANCED OUT THE BIG picture window and saw a dogcatcher's truck pull up in front of the diner. The customers had almost cleared out for the day and I was watching the clock. I had found an old recipe for apple pie and I wanted to get home and give it a try. I was going to have to hit the gym a little harder if I wanted to keep the weight off while I worked on this cookbook. It was one of the hazards of the profession.

Gary Dunning walked through the door and I smiled at him.

"Hi Gary," I said as I wiped down one of the tables.

"Hi Rainey," he said with a grin. "I thought I'd stop in for a little something to tide me over until dinner. Just don't tell my wife."

"No problem," I said and walked toward him. "Do you have anything particular in mind?"

I was a little disappointed he had chosen that moment to come in. With it being nearly closing time we were trying to get things cleaned up for the next day, but we would stay open as long as there were customers. Working at a diner that only served breakfast and lunch had its advantages though. Even if customers wandered in close to closing, we never stayed open much past 3:00.

"How about a cup of coffee and a piece of whatever you have that's sweet?" he asked and headed toward the front counter. "I'll just sit here and not mess up a table. I know it's close to closing."

"It's no problem, Gary. We have lemon merengue pie and some chocolate cake left," I said and went behind the counter.

"How about that pie?" he said. "I love lemon."

"Coming right up," I said and put an empty coffee cup and a place setting in front of him. "How are you doing today?"

I filled the cup with coffee and turned to the display dish and cut him a piece of the pie.

"Pretty good. The weather's nice today," he said. "Hey Rainey, I wanted to let you know that we got in the cutest red dachshund puppy yesterday. I know you mentioned having one as a kid when you came in with your nieces."

"Really?" I asked, my ears perking up. "I've had it on my mind since we went to see the puppies at the shelter. Tell me about the puppy."

"It's a little girl and she looks to be about ten weeks old. Could be a couple weeks older than that, but she's still pretty young. I bet your nieces would love to have her to play with when they visit their auntie."

I chuckled and put a plate with a piece of pie on it in front of him. "They would love that. I always thought I'd get another one, but I wasn't exactly looking for one right now."

"Oh?" he asked, picking up his fork. "What were you doing at the shelter, then?"

"Oh," I said, realizing I had just made a mistake. "I thought it would be fun to bring the girls to look at the puppies. They would love one, but I'm afraid their father is allergic."

"I see," he said with a nod of his head. "Well, that makes it doubly important that their auntie has one they can come and visit then, doesn't it? Every kid needs a dog and if they can't have one at their own house, then someone needs to step up and keep one at their house for them." He said it with a chuckle and a knowing look.

"You're right. Every kid needs a dog. Or a cat. We had both when Stormy and I were kids. It seemed we were never without a pet," I said thoughtfully. "Maybe I'll take a look."

"Well, don't wait too long. She's awfully cute. Someone will adopt her right out from under you."

I nodded, thinking it over. "I'll think about it. I promise."

I DIDN'T GO TO THE shelter right after work. I had a pie to work on. The grocery store was my first stop to pick up the ingredients for the pie. Apple pie wouldn't be too difficult to make in larger quantities to add temporarily to the diner menu. If I could come up with some changes and tweaks to the recipe I had found, I was sure it would be a hit. I felt confident that it would sell well and I was going to approach Sam with the idea when I had perfected the recipe.

After I got home, I quickly put the pie together and popped it in the oven. Then I remembered the puppy. It was after five o'clock and I was sure the shelter would be closed. We didn't need a puppy. A puppy needed to be trained, and I didn't know if Poofy would get along with one. Poofy was set in her ways as most cats are.

I was headed to my room when I decided to stop by the shelter, anyway. Maybe someone would still be around. I couldn't get the picture of a cute red dachshund puppy out of my head.

"Mom, can you watch the pie I just put in the oven?" I asked her. "I set the timer for it."

"Sure, dear. Where are you going?" she asked from her place on the sofa.

"It's a surprise," I said.

She groaned. "You and your surprises."

THE SIGN OUT FRONT on the shelter said closed, but I parked and got out of my car, anyway. I could see that the office lights were still on and when I tried the door, it was unlocked so I went in. The office was empty.

"Hello?" I called.

There was no answer, so I pushed open the swinging doors that separated the office from the shelter area where the animals were kept.

"Hello? Gary?" I called. The dogs started barking when I spoke, making a din that made it hard to hear anything else. I looked into the kennel the girls and I had looked at the other day. The puppies were excited to see me, but I didn't see a red dachshund among them. I noted that several of them that had been here the other day were gone. That made me feel good. The puppies now had good homes instead of living at the shelter.

I squatted down next to the gate of the kennel and stuck my fingers through the chain link. I was rewarded with six little pink tongues licking my fingers as the puppies jockeyed for position. I chuckled. "You guys are too cute."

I looked up and saw Gary approaching from across the room. I stood up and smiled at him.

Gary gave me a smile that looked more sinister than sweet. That was when I realized I had made a mistake.

Chapter Seventeen

"RAINEY, I DIDN'T THINK you'd show up so soon," Gary said, advancing on me at a fast pace. "It's good to see you."

"I thought I'd check out that little dachshund you mentioned earlier," I said, hesitating. Something about him made the hair on the back of my neck stand up. He held one hand behind him and something about his demeanor had changed since earlier in the day.

He smiled. "Come on back and I'll show him to you," he said, motioning with his free hand toward a backroom.

"Him?" I questioned.

"Yes, the little dachshund. Don't worry, the dogs won't get out of their cages," he said when I still hesitated.

It wasn't the dogs I was hesitant about. "You said the dachshund was a girl," I pointed out.

"Oh, that's right. It is a girl. I was thinking about another puppy we got in this afternoon. Sorry, I got confused."

"Oh," I said, nodding. "Okay, sure. Where is she?"

He nodded toward the backroom again. "She's back here. I kept her aside for you to take a look. Like I said earlier, dachshunds go quickly, and I didn't want someone else to adopt her before you had a chance to look at her."

Something told me not to go in that room, but I wasn't sure why. I started walking with him and felt in my front jeans pocket to make sure my phone was still there.

The closer we got to the door, the surer I was that I shouldn't go in that room.

"You know, maybe I should bring my mother here to make sure she's okay with getting a puppy," I said, stopping in my tracks. "I'm still living with her and she has a cat. If the cat doesn't get along with the puppy, it would be disastrous. I'll just come back tomorrow and bring her with me."

That was when he took hold of my arm, squeezing tightly. "Let's go have a look at her now. Like I said, she'll go quickly and you don't want to lose her to someone else," he said, forcing me forward.

"Gary, let go of me," I said sternly and jerked my arm away.

"I said, we're going to have a look at her," he said through clenched teeth. He grabbed for me again and I stepped back, swinging my purse at his head. I was glad that I carried a large purse filled with an assortment of items that I never needed before now. Their combined weight made my purse a good weapon.

When my purse made contact with his head, he raised a hand to shield himself, but it was too late. The purse made contact with a thud. He groaned and swore at me, turning his head with the swing of the purse. The hand he had kept behind his back held a monkey wrench and he lost his grip on it when he put his hand to his head. I turned and ran for the door I had come in without looking back.

My running excited the dogs, and they barked louder as they strained against their enclosures. To them, it probably looked like we were having fun and they wanted to join in, but I had never been more terrified than at that moment.

Gary grabbed me from behind and I screamed as he spun me around.

"You are one nosy little know-it-all and you are not getting involved in my business," he said, gripping my arm tightly. "You should have minded your own business."

I tried to swing at him with my purse again, but he was too close to me. "Let me go, Gary!" I yelled.

"Nope," he said and dragged me toward the backroom again. "You are not giving me away."

I grabbed his arm and dug my manicured nails in. He screamed in pain and I felt my nails dig into flesh as he tried to force my hand loose. I took that moment to give him an uppercut to his throat, and he stumbled back, clutching at it. I vowed to renew my membership at the gym as soon as I got away from him. Those kickboxing lessons were paying off.

I turned to run, but slipped in a puddle of water on the concrete, landing with a solid thud. Pain shot through my hip and elbow and I lay stunned for a moment. Gary came at me, with one hand still on his throat. His face had turned bright red, and he wheezed as he kicked me in the ribs. I heard a crack and pain coursed through my body. Everything began to turn black, and I inhaled deeply, trying to fight off unconsciousness.

Every dog in the place was barking at the top of their lungs and above it all, I heard a deep-throated baying. I turned my head and saw a blue tick hound frantically barking at us. The door to the kennel she was in was open a crack and a garden hose lay on the ground near it. The water trailed from where the hose lay to where it puddled. That was what I had slipped in.

The pain in my body kept me from doing anything other than dragging myself toward the kennel.

"You aren't getting away," Gary said, breathing hard as he reached for my leg.

I rolled over and used my good leg to kick at Gary with all my strength, hitting him in the shin. Pain from my ribs and my injured hip made me cry out.

The doors on these kennels slid open instead of swinging and I hooked my fingers into the chain link door, hoping the hound dog was going to be on my side. She stuck her wet nose against my fingers as I pushed the gate with all my might, sliding it just wide enough for her to get out.

The dog growled and jumped on Gary, sinking her teeth into his arm as he tried to shield himself. He cried out, and I shoved my hand into my pocket for my phone.

Trying to get the 911 operator to hear me above the barking and Gary's screaming was a challenge, but I managed to ask for a policeman before the room started spinning and I blacked out.

Chapter Eighteen

I WAS SPRAWLED ON THE sofa with a diet Pepsi and a bowl of popcorn, watching an old black and white Perry Mason show when the doorbell rang.

"Mom!" I called without making a move. Being out of commission had its benefits. I could lie on the couch while my mother waited on me.

"I got it," she said, heading to the front door. "Seems like I've been waiting on you all your life."

"And I appreciate it so much," I assured her.

In my defense, I had three broken ribs and a bruised hip from my mishap with Gary Dunning. It would have taken me at least fifteen minutes just to get off the sofa. I was doing us both a favor by allowing her to get it.

"She's right here, Cade," I heard my mother say.

I gasped and tried to sit up. My ribs screamed at me and I groaned in pain and decided against it. He would just have to see me without any makeup and messy hair.

"Well, good evening," he said as my mother led him to where I lay.

I felt self-conscious in my old t-shirt and ratty sweats, but there was nothing I could do about it now.

"Hi," I said. "Would you like some popcorn?" I held the bowl out to him.

"I'm fine, thanks. I just thought I'd check up on you," he said and took the chair Mom offered him. "How are you feeling?"

"I've been better. Everything seems to hurt. I'd sit up to talk to you, but honestly, I don't think I can," I said weakly.

"That's okay. I understand completely. Who are your friends?" he asked, looking at Poofy, who was sitting on the back of the sofa and Maggie, my new blue tick hound laying on the floor in front of the sofa.

"The cat is Poofy, and the dog is Maggie," I said. "I had to spring Maggie out of doggie jail. She saved my life after all."

At the sound of her name, Maggie wagged her tail, thumping it on the hardwood floor.

He grinned. "She definitely did save your life. Thanks to her, Gary Dunning is still in the hospital."

"Ew, that bad, huh?" I asked. I had blacked out and missed what had happened to him, but I knew Maggie had handled the situation as only she could.

He nodded. "Maggie used his arm as a chew toy. Don't worry though, he'll live. He's scheduled to be released in the morning and they have a nice bed for him at the county jail where he can finish his recovery."

"I'm not worried," I said. "He's lucky to be alive. Carlisle didn't have the same luck."

"No, he sure didn't," he agreed.

"Can I get you something to drink, Cade?" Mom asked.

"No thank you Mrs. Daye, I'm fine," he said.

Mom was getting familiar with him. I still felt like I didn't know him well enough to call him anything other than detective. But then, Mom had never met a stranger. She could carry on a conversation with a statue.

"Did he confess?" I asked the detective.

"After some persuasion, yes. He was jealous of Carlisle. According to him, Carlisle liked to rub his nose in his failures. He said Carlisle had done it all his life and he just couldn't take it anymore."

"So, Carlisle's promotion was the last straw?" I asked him as Maggie put her nose on the edge of the sofa. I reached over and scratched it.

"So it would seem. He said he and Carlisle were working late and Carlisle came over to him and rubbed his nose in it one more time. He said that was the last straw and he couldn't take it anymore. Gary had been working on a leaky faucet and there was a large wrench lying nearby. He said he didn't mean to do it, but rage from all his past failures took over and he hit him in the head."

I rolled my eyes. "And I guess he accidentally took him to the river to get rid of his body?"

He chuckled. "Accidents happen."

"Well, it was no accident that he lured me to the shelter to get rid of me," I pointed out. "There wasn't even a dachshund puppy there."

I was still put out by the fact that the puppy didn't exist. She and Maggie would have been a fine addition to our household.

"No, it wasn't an accident. He had plans for you. Even though the shelter is now a no-kill shelter, the drug used to euthanize animals was still there at the shelter. That's why he wanted you in that back room. That's where it was kept."

I winced. "How horrible." It shocked me that someone could think like that, let alone try to carry it out. I patted Maggie's head to make myself feel better.

"If you'll recall, I did warn you not to get involved in things that didn't concern you," he said gently.

I sighed. "I know. It was stupid. But once I started talking to people, I just couldn't stop. I kind of like puzzles."

It was his turn to sigh. "Murder isn't a puzzle. You need to leave solving murders to the professionals."

"I'll try to do that in the future," I said.

"You had better try very hard," he said a little more forcefully.

"Fine."

I knew he was right. I should have shut my mouth and minded my own business. I don't know why I just couldn't seem to do that.

"How does Poofy like her new fur sister?" he asked.

Poofy twitched her tail and looked at him when she heard her name.

"She's much better about it than I had thought she would be. The first couple of days they were wary of each other, but I found them snuggled together on Maggie's bed this morning. I think they'll get along just fine."

"That's good news," he said. "Too bad about the puppy. They would have made a cute threesome."

I chuckled. "They sure would."

I took a deep breath and looked at him from where I lay on the sofa. Cade Starkey was a puzzle himself. He could be so distant. Cold, even. And then other times he could be so human.

I was pretty sure that I still disliked him. But maybe I disliked him a little less than I had before.

The End

Sneak Peek

CHERRY PIE AND A MURDER

A Rainey Daye Cozy Mystery, book 3

Chapter One

"Some people have no consideration for others," I grumbled to myself as I loaded my arms with dirty dishes. One of the other waitresses at Sam's Diner, Georgia Johnson, had skipped out on work today. Again. I felt tired, rushed, and cranky as I was left to handle more customers than one person could manage. But at least Luanne Merrill was here doing her part. Luanne was a good waitress and Sam's wasn't a big diner, but what we lacked in size, we made up for in volume. With three waitresses on duty, we could just handle the mid-week lunchtime crowds. When we were short a person, things got pretty crazy.

"Can I get some ketchup?" a woman near the back of the diner called.

"I'll get that for you right now," I called back, forcing myself to smile. A shock of my long blond hair had slipped out of my purple hair tie and I pushed it behind my ear. My hair was getting too long and out of control and I needed a trim, but there was no time to worry about that now.

I hurried to the kitchen to get the ketchup, hoping I wouldn't let any of the dishes in my arms slip and crash to the floor.

"Busy out there?" Sam asked as he flipped a burger, barely glancing in my direction. At thirty-eight, Sam was three years older than me and had medium brown hair that had gotten shaggy in the past few weeks.

"It's crazy out there. Where's Georgia?" I asked and gently set the dishes on the sideboard near the sink. "Sorry to do this to you, Ron."

Ron White was our dishwasher. The faded tattoo of the hula girl on his bicep shimmered as he snorted and picked up the stack of dishes I had just set down. He placed them in the deep stainless steel sink full of sudsy water. "I live for dirty dishes."

"I haven't heard from Georgia today," Sam said nonchalantly. He leaned away from the grill as fat from the hamburger patties dripped down into the fire and popped and sizzled. The flames momentarily flared up and then settled down again.

I sighed and picked up a bottle of ketchup from the counter where Sam set the orders that waited to be taken out to the tables.

"Really Sam? How many times has she done this? It's got to be at least three times this month alone," I said in exasperation.

Georgia and I had issues. She was on me all the time, complaining about everything I did, and I wasn't going to let this go easily.

"Now, Rainey," Sam said in a tone that sounded like he was trying to soothe a child. "It's been a while since she completely skipped out on work. You know she has some family issues to deal with."

"Sam, she's late all the time. And when she isn't late, she's got a rotten attitude," I protested. Georgia's family issues consisted of a husband that didn't like to work. Sure, that must be stressful, but it seemed like that would make her try harder to be here and keep her job, not make her want to skip out on it. But Georgia did as she pleased and she had a history of doing this.

"I know, I know," Sam said without looking at me. "I've got a couple of orders ready to go." He nodded at the two plates of burgers and fries he had just set down on the counter for my tables.

"Got it," I said with another melodramatic sigh. If anyone else had skipped out on work, I would have been more understanding, but Georgia was my nemesis. I couldn't find it in me to be kind. I shifted the ketchup bottle to the crook of my arm, then added another, and then picked up the two plates. When you waitressed, you learned to multi-task.

Sam was a laid-back boss. I had no complaints about him, except maybe when he allowed certain people to get away with murder. I chided myself to shut my mouth about it. Or at least, try to. I occasionally needed him to show me some kindness when I occasionally came in late. I didn't want him to point that out.

"Here we are, Ladies," I said as I set the plates and a bottle of ketchup on table seven. "The best burgers in Sparrow. Can I get you anything else?"

"No, thank you," the older woman said. "These look so good."

"You won't be disappointed," I assured her. "You let me know if I can do anything else for you. And don't forget, we have triple-layer chocolate cake on the dessert menu."

"I was thinking about that," the younger woman said. "I might have to give it a try."

"I highly recommend it," I said with a smile and headed back to table twelve with the other bottle of ketchup.

In a former life, I had done the cooking segments on a New York morning talk show and written best-selling cookbooks. But a nasty divorce had landed me back in my hometown of Sparrow, Idaho and working part-time for Sam's Diner. I loved the diner and most of my co-workers, Georgia Johnson excepted, but I was working on another cookbook and hoping it would be a breakout book that would allow me to be financially stable enough to move out of my mother's house and into one of my own. Sam had graciously allowed me to try out recipes on customers and I was taking advantage of his kindness. It was a great way to get feedback on my recipes.

"Hi there, sorry for the delay," I said to the middle-aged woman at table twelve. I set the bottle of ketchup down and noticed she had already eaten half her fries. "Is there something else I can get for you?"

She narrowed her eyes at me. "What's the point in bringing the ketchup now? I'm almost finished."

"I'm so sorry," I said. And I was. I hated disappointing people. "Can I make it up to you by offering you a piece of triple-layer chocolate cake? On the house?"

She brightened at the mention of the cake. "Well, I really shouldn't, but since it's on the house, that would be very nice of you. Thank you."

I smiled. "It's a new recipe. If I can get your opinion on it, it would help me to perfect the recipe. Will you do that for me?"

She nodded, having forgotten her rancor at having missed out on ketchup for her fries. "I can do that."

"Great, I'll be right back with the cake."

I headed back to the kitchen to get the cake, glancing at the tables as I left. Table nine needed a refill on iced tea and table ten would need their bill soon.

Once back in the kitchen, I lifted the cover on the chocolate cake. The scent of chocolate wafted up, and I inhaled. There was no more perfect smell on this earth than chocolate.

"How's it going out there? Everyone happy?" Sam asked me without turning around.

"Yes, everything's good. A couple of the tables have been vacated and I predict we should get out of here no later than 3:30." Working at a diner that was only open for breakfast and lunch had its advantages.

"Sounds great to me," Ron said as he rinsed the huge stainless steel pot that Sam used to make clam chowder in.

I cut a slice of the cake, put it on a plate and got a fork. "I hope this cake is as good as it smells."

"I had a small piece earlier, Rainey," Ron said. "It's very good. Reminds me of my grandma's."

Now that was what I wanted to hear. My new cookbook was going to have an Americana theme and if it was as good as grandma's—anyone's grandma—then I was on the right track. "Thanks, Ron, I'm happy you liked it," I said and headed out to the dining room with the cake. People turned to look at the plate I held as I passed with the cake and I smiled. I had a feeling it was going to sell out shortly.

The rest of the afternoon passed quickly. Yet another benefit of working in a busy diner. You didn't have time to watch the clock when you were running back and forth to serve customers.

Later, when the diner had cleared out, I went to the front door and locked it with a sigh of relief. My feet ached, and I was more than ready to go home and put them up. The chocolate cake had sold out, as predicted, and everyone that I had a chance to speak to about it had deemed it a success. It made me feel good, but I knew I would still feel the need to tweak the recipe. I was a perfectionist and I couldn't help but try to make it as wonderful as possible.

"Oh, my aching feet," Luanne groaned as she put dirty dishes into a rubber basin to carry back to Ron.

"Mine too," I agreed. "Today was crazier than usual. It would have been nice if Georgia had shown up and given us a hand."

She nodded. "Poor Georgia doesn't know what she missed. Tips were really good today."

And they had been. On busy days like this, I had to keep reminding myself of all the good things about working here so

I wouldn't miss the morning show I used to appear on. I had been semi-famous in New York. Now I was only known locally because I had grown up in Sparrow.

I got my own rubber container and began filling it with dirty dishes. Sam said the diner wasn't big enough to have a busboy, but I wished we had one at least during the summer months when the tourists showed up. The Snake River ran just outside of town and it was a popular travel destination.

"I liked your chocolate cake. Maybe next time you can make a cherry one. Cherry is my favorite," Luanne said, brushing her short brown hair away from her forehead.

My eyebrows furrowed in thought. Cherry cake. I couldn't remember making one before and it was something to think about.

"I just might do that," I said, picking up some glasses from the table I was cleaning.

There was a frantic tapping on the diner's glass door and I looked over. Georgia stood there, over-sized black handbag over her shoulder, tapping her key on the glass. When she saw me looking in her direction, she frantically waved me over. I frowned. Now was a great time to show up, I thought. I sighed and slid my feet across the floor and over to the door, not in any hurry to let her in. What was the point of coming to work now?

I turned the key in the door and pushed it open a few inches. "Nice of you to show up now, Georgia. If I were you, I'd be ashamed to come here and show my face after you skipped out on work."

She looked at me wide-eyed. "Someone murdered my Uncle Donald."

Buy Cherry Pie and a Murder on Amazon:

https://www.amazon.com/gp/product/B07DR981Z5

If you'd like updates on the newest books I'm writing, follow me on Amazon and Facebook:

https://www.facebook.com/Kathleen-Suzette-Kate-Bell-authors-759206390932120/

https://www.amazon.com/Kathleen-Suzette/e/B07B7D2S4W/ref=dp_byline_cont_pop_ebooks_1